LETTER TO MY LOVE

They had met at a dance, met once or twice by appointment afterwards – and then he had flown to Canada and she had gone on looking after her father, reading to him, sitting with him, taking him for slow, short walks or for slow, short drives. She had not forgotten the quiet, shy man with the fair hair and grey eyes and unemphatic way of speaking, and Grant Hewitt had been unable to forget the lovely, slender girl and her grace and her laughter. There had been letters. Claire, looking across the room at the grave, moody man by the window, wondered whether she had imagined the warm, passionate sentences, the bridge of love and longing that he had flung across an ocean. He had come back, they had become engaged ...

Letter To My Love

Elizabeth Cadell

CORONET BOOKS
Hodder Paperbacks Ltd., London

Copyright © 1963 by Elizabeth Cadell
First published by Hodder and Stoughton Ltd
1963
Coronet edition 1970
Second impression 1975

Printed and bound in Great Britain for Coronet Books,
Hodder Paperbacks Ltd., St. Paul's House, Warwick Lane,
London EC4P 4AH, by Cox & Wyman Ltd, London,
Reading and Fakenham

ISBN 0 340 10881 9

CHAPTER ONE

THE market town of Gisborough is situated in one of the less picturesque parts of Sussex. Although only a mile or two off the main London–Brighton road, it has a deserted, dispirited air, except on Thursday mornings, when stalls laden with fruit and vegetables appear on the square, giving it a colourful, almost Continental look. For a few hours, the streets and car parks become crowded and busy; the town's only hotel enjoys a brief lunch-time prosperity – but by mid-afternoon, all is quiet once more; the car-park attendant and the hotel porter are left to count their tips and look forward to next Thursday, or to the only other likely source of revenue: a wedding.

On a rainy afternoon in May, a wedding reception was being held in the hotel dining-room – but the porter, after running an experienced eye over the sparse assembly, decided that this was not the kind of wedding from which he could reap any substantial harvest. The guests were middle-aged or elderly, the bridegroom's two sisters were on their last legs, and there had been no speeches, no toasts, none of the conviviality that led to a loosening of purse strings. You couldn't, he summed up, carrying out the suitcases and placing himself in a strategic position by the door of the bridal car, call it a wedding at all, with a bride and bridegroom of that age.

The bridegroom was sixty-four, and had a grown-up daughter named Claire, who, with her fiancé, had given the sole touch of youth to the occasion. The bride was forty-one, and had been, before today's ceremony, Miss Margaret Swithin, Matron of the Gisborough Cottage Hospital. Now Mrs. Edwin Marston, she was considered by her husband's two aged sisters, Netta and Ettie, who had not previously met her, to have won a valuable matrimonial prize, and they had come to the wedding in Queen Alexandra collars and Queen Mary toques with the hope of seeing in the bride a proper appreciation of her good fortune. By the end of the afternoon they had learned that she was a woman of dignity and of such sound good sense, that they were obliged to concede that some of the luck was on Edwin's side. Having settled this matter, they turned their attention to the other reason that had brought them to the wedding: namely, to discover what was holding up the wedding of their niece Claire.

They had, in the intervals of scrutinizing the bride, endeavoured to form some opinion of Claire's fiancé, Grant Hewitt. Outwardly, Netta told Ettie, he looked sound enough. She paused, waved aside the champagne and gave a quavering but authoritative order for lemonade. She was tall and upright and had straight, scanty, iron-grey hair and her voice, in her youth, had been loud and commanding; it had subdued a great many people, including her long-dead husband. At eighty-three, the bugle note was cracked, and attempts to browbeat eighty-year-old Ettie were further defeated by the latter's increasing tendency to slip away into a region inhabited entirely by ghosts.

"He's not tall, but he's well-built, Ettie. He's not handsome, but he's got a steady look."

"Yes, dear." Ettie, small and dessicated, had a dried-up wisp of a voice. Her tiny face was framed in fluffy, woolly white hair; her eyes, even now, were a tender blue. "How fast Claire's growing."

"Claire isn't growing. Claire's twenty-six. Are you listening to what I'm saying?"

"Of course. Go on with it, whatever it was."

"It was about her fiancé. I don't know why we worried so much. I still don't understand the reason for this long postponement, but you can see he's very much in love with her."

"Then what," enquired Ettie, "can it be?"

"What can what be?"

"Delay, you said. You said he must be slippery."

"If I did, which I doubt, I was wrong. I simply pointed out that he was thirty-one, with a house of his own and a good deal of money. You've only to look at him to see that he's in splendid health – so why this hanging about? They became engaged in January and now we're into May. There was, of course, the unfortunate business of his mother's death – a pity it got into the newspapers – but that was at the beginning of February. So – Ettie, you're not attending."

"Yes, indeed. You were saying that you liked Grant very much."

"What I said was that he seems to me quite reliable, but he looks as though there's something weighing on his mind."

"Oh really?" fluted Ettie. "What, exactly?"

"How should I know?"

"But surely he should know?"

"Most certainly Claire should know."

"Or," said Ettie with one of her rare flashes of lucidity, "we should know."

"Quite so. We must do something. Edwin can't be expected to deal with a situation of this kind."

Claire Marston, studying her two aunts across the room, was well aware of both the reasons that had brought them down, at such great effort, from their comfortable flat in London. She had managed, so far, to avoid the traps they had set for her; now, seated in a quiet corner, they waited with a vacant seat between them, signalling to her to join them.

"I suppose," she said to Grant, "I'd better get it over."

"I don't see why."

His tone, seldom other than calm, held resentment, and she turned to look at him. So he'd noticed, she thought, relief flooding her mind. He'd noticed. For her, the afternoon had been charged with the guests' unspoken conjectures: what was holding up her wedding? Everybody present was aware that she was to have been married in March; everybody knew that her father's marriage had for

8

a time waited upon her own. Beneath today's courtesies and congratulations there had been an undercurrent of keen speculation: could something be wrong? Claire, sensitive to atmosphere, had not expected Grant to show any awareness; she knew him to be lacking in imagination and perhaps in perception. Now, with gratitude, she realized that the unspoken criticism had found its way into his consciousness and had made him, for the first time in the past uneasy months, study their situation from a detached point of view.

"I've got to talk to them," she said. "You ought to come too."

"I'd much rather not."

Without further urging, she left him and walked over to join the two fragile old figures, and as always, the sight of them sent her feelings swinging between affection and pity and deep, impotent rage at the ravages that time had wrought in them. She could not remember them as other than aged and withered, but she knew that they had once been beautiful; old photographs proved it, as well as the legends that still persisted in their native village of Hallowes. Netta had married at nineteen; Ettie had remained single only because she had found it impossible to choose any one of the brilliant young men at her feet. The two sisters had been renowned for their dazzling complexions and their vitality and their hour-glass figures, and Claire could not bear to see what they had become. If life divided itself into seven ages or stages, she thought, taking the vacant chair, she herself would prefer to slip away before this last lamentable one.

"Claire dear," Netta began without preamble, "we've just been having a little talk about you. You mustn't think us interfering old women; you must remember that there's really nobody but ourselves to keep an eye on you. You can't expect your father, with his precarious health, to—"

The end of the sentence was lost on Claire, whose mind had fixed on the word precarious. Uncertain, doubtful. Could sixty-four years without actual illness, with no undue discomfort, come under the heading of precarious health? Her mother had undoubtedly thought so; she had throughout her married life accorded her husband the status of a semi-invalid. Before her, Netta and Ettie had thought so too; they had looked after their brother until his marriage. After her, the duty, or the privilege, had passed to Claire. She was aware that she had not shown the skill and devotion of her predecessors, and her father's decision to avail himself of more efficient ministrations had not surprised her.

Surprise had in any case been ruled out from the first by Miss Swithin's open, disarmingly candid courtship. Mr. Marston had felt, a few months after his wife's death, that time was failing to exercise its proverbial healing powers, and he had decided to go for treatment to the hospital at Gisborough, which had a wide and well-deserved reputation for the treatment of nervous cases. Claire drove him the eight intervening miles; Miss Swithin received him and might be said never to have given him back. She had, on his return home, promised to drive over to Hallowes and see how he was getting on; her little black car had become a familiar sight passing through the little village and entering the tall gates, and it had stood for many hours outside the graceful white house. Claire, waiting month after month for her fiancé to agree to a definite date for their own wedding, had watched with envy the cool, firm manner in which Margaret Swithin had handled her elderly suitor. Edwin Marston needed her, and she knew that she could make him happy; these facts being established, nothing remained but to bring about a union. This she had done; today she stood in her neat grey suit beside her husband, ready to protect and cherish him as his sisters and his first wife and his daughter had protected and cherished him. Good sense, good judgment, quiet, unobtrusive firmness – these qualities she had demonstrated clearly. She had used them on her own behalf, and Claire was longing to see them directed to her own problems. But the wedding preparations had left little time in which to approach her future stepmother, even if she had known how to phrase an appeal for help. The only counsellors she had were these two tottering old ladies from whom she realized her attention had wandered.

" – holding up the wedding, Claire dear. It can't," Netta pointed out, "be on account of his mother's death. That was a dreadful thing, of course, but young couples don't put off marrying indefinitely if there's a family bereavement; they simply postpone the wedding for a short while, and marry quietly. So – Ettie, may we have your attention?"

Ettie, to Claire's relief, was not interested in the present.

"Surely" – she leaned across to Netta – "that's Grace Hall over there?"

"Grace Hall," Netta said, "is dead."

"Are you sure?"

"Perfectly sure. She died over fifteen years ago, and we went to her funeral."

"In that case," Ettie conceded, "she cannot be sitting over there. Unless . . ."

"About the delay," pursued Netta. "We understand that your fiancé inherited everything under his mother's Will – house, money, everything. There were no bequests?"

"None."

"But I understand from your father that there are some people living in the house, who refuse to leave."

"Grant hasn't asked them to leave," said Claire.

"Who are they? Relations?"

"One is Grant's stepsister, Lotty."

"Stepsister? Grant's mother was married more than once?"

"Yes. Her name was Mrs. Tennant. She was a widow for a long time. Then, about eight years ago, she married someone who had a grown-up son and daughter."

"A great mistake," Ettie said. "Don't you remember poor Mary Tresser, Netta? She married a man with four children, and he died and left everything to them and poor Mary was left with nothing."

"She was left with a nice little income. What her stepchildren got was simply what had belonged to their own mother. Now, Claire: this Lotty you mentioned; she's not the only one living in the house?"

"No. There's her little boy, and a housekeeper."

"Little boy? She's married?"

"She's a widow."

"What's her name?"

"Mrs. Summerhill."

"I knew a Summerhill once," Ettie said. "I wonder if she'd be any relation? That girl who used to stay with the Howeys, Netta – do you remember?"

"Her name was Summerley. Claire—"

"She ran away with somebody – an actor. Not a good actor."

"Ettie, would you very kindly stop interrupting when I'm trying to talk to Claire? Now, Claire: Mrs. Summerhill and her little boy and a housekeeper. Who else?"

"Nobody – except an old gardener. I saw them all when I went down to the funeral."

"I suppose you had met Grant's mother?"

"No. Grant and I had arranged to go down there just after we became engaged, but she died before I could meet her."

"No girl of my generation," said Neta, "would have dreamed of accepting a man until she had met his family. I'm sorry to see the old rules being brushed aside. I can quite see why your father kept us in the dark about his decision to remarry: we would only have worried about him – quite unnecessarily, as it turns out. But you should have brought Grant to see us. We are, after all, your nearest relations. And you should have gone down to meet his mother before you became engaged."

"There wasn't time," Claire explained. "As you know, Grant and I met in September, just before his firm sent him to Canada for four months. He—"

She paused. September . . .

They had met at a dance, met once or twice by appointment afterwards – and then he had flown to Canada and she had gone on looking after her father, reading to him, sitting with him, taking him for slow, short walks or for slow, short drives. She had not forgotten the quiet, shy man with the fair hair and grey eyes and unemphatic way of speaking, and Grant Hewitt had been unable to forget the lovely, slender girl and her grace and her laughter. There had been letters. Claire, looking across the room at the grave, moody man by the window, wondered whether she had imagined the warm, passionate sentences, the bridge of love and longing that he had flung across an ocean. He had come back, they had become engaged . . .

"So she died before you could meet her?" Netta was saying.

"She fell down a flight of stairs at the lawyer's office, just after making a new Will," said Ettie. "I read about it. The same thing happened to poor Trixie Mayhew. But she didn't die."

"She did die," Netta said.

"No, Netta. She broke a leg and—"

"She died of pneumonia nearly twenty years ago."

"Did we go to her funeral?"

"No, we didn't."

"Then how can you be sure—"

"She died in Hong Kong. What I want to know, Claire, is whether it's this Will that's causing the delay."

"In a way, yes," Claire said.

"Hitch in it?" Ettie asked. "I remember being left two thousand pounds by my poor godmother, but the hitch was that by the time she died, she'd spent all the legacies."

"This Will," Claire said, "was quite in order."

"Then somebody must talk to this young man," Netta said with as much decision as her quavering tones could command. "If this goes on, you'll wake up and find yourself an old woman, like me."

"Or single, like me," said Ettie.

"Would you like me to talk to him?" Netta asked.

"No, thank you, Aunt Netta. I wouldn't," Claire answered.

But somebody, she thought, would soon have to say something. She had gone down with Grant to his mother's funeral. Nobody in the circumstances could have been expected to be in a cheerful frame of mind, but after the reading of the Will – at which she was not present – he had turned without warning into the silent, morose man she had known for the past three months. The house he loved – Spenders House, on the outskirts of the Kentish town of the same name – the house about which he had told her so much, was now his, but he had from that day onwards made no attempt to outline his future plans, and had refused to go down to the house to discuss the situation with his stepsister or with his mother's housekeeper. Claire had not at first pressed him; the terms of the Will had left him in a difficult position, and he was not a man capable of making swift decisions. But February had given way to March and April and May, and still the mere mention of the Will brought the same reactions; it had never, he protested over and over again, been meant by his mother to be her last; she would never have gone back on all her promises, never have left old servants unrewarded.

"But you offered to help them all, Grant," she had pointed out.

"And they refused, and I don't blame them. My mother never made any secret of what she was going to leave them; it was all drawn up years ago; we all knew what we could expect. And then . . ."

"If you went down again now, after they've all had time to think things over——"

"Not now, Claire. Later."

Perhaps the coming of spring, she thought, had caused her change of mood. She had begun by sympathizing with his desire to keep away from the house; to go down too soon might have appeared too strong a hint to those still occupying it. She had admired his patience and his feelings of delicacy and she could not decide exactly when she had come to believe that his refusal to act, to move, to come to any kind of decision was the result not of consideration, but of cowardice. The house was his, and he lacked the courage to claim it.

She came back to the present to find that her father

and stepmother were beside them. Edwin looked down at his two sisters.

"Well, are you tired, you girls?" he asked.

Coming from anybody else, Claire reflected, the words would have had a facetious sound – but her father had never made a facetious remark in his life, and if he had, her mother would have missed the humour. Where her own spring of gaiety, her own love of laughter came from, she was unable to decide; probably from Ettie.

She looked at her stepmother, trim and neat, the grey suit given a bridal touch by an orchid, a lacy white hat and white gloves, and wondered how much happiness she expected. From the hospital to a life devoted to this tall, handsome, white-haired, semi-professional invalid. Not for the first time, Claire tried to assess what it was about her father that had ensured him loving and lifelong service. He asked nothing; there had never been any need to ask. He accepted gravely, gently, gratefully the ministrations of sisters, wife, daughter and faithful old servants. Perhaps, she thought, it was the touch of the saint or the sage or the scholar in his appearance; he drew disciples. Claire did not think that he had ever suffered, but he had the air of one who would suffer in silence.

She had learned, since her mother's death, that the scholarly look hid an almost limitless vapidity of mind. The classics that filled the bookshelves in his room, the impressive works that lay on the table beside his easy chair, the serious new literature regularly ordered from book-sellers – all these, she now knew, were part of the picture, but if her father had ever had intellect, it had atrophied; if he had ever had initiative or ambition, it had been smothered beneath invalid rugs or drowned in nourishing beverages. At sixty-four, his sweetness remained undiminished by suffering, his natural gentleness unruffled by opposition. And this new wife, Claire realized with a certainty that sent her already warm feeling for her close to love, would do nothing to jar or to interrupt the smooth flow of service. Edwin Marston was indeed in luck.

"If you're going up to change," she asked her, "can I come and help?"

"Come by all means" – her stepmother ushered her towards the lift – "but I'm not changing. All I'm doing is removing this orchid and this hat and these high-heeled shoes, which I can't bear any longer."

She and Claire went up to the neat, impersonal room she had occupied since leaving the hospital two weeks ago. Having no home of her own, she had arranged to be married from the Gisborough hotel, with a married couple, distant cousins, to act as host and hostess.

The room was small, but the windows overlooked the river, on to which the sun was sending flickering, tree-patterned reflections. Flowers – the bridegroom's daily message to his bride – stood in tall vases on dressing-table, writing-table and mantelpiece, and to these Mrs. Marston directed Claire's attention.

"It's such a shame to leave them here," she said. "Would you have time to take them to a patient at the hospital?"

"Of course. Will you write a card?"

Mrs. Marston wrote one and placed it beside a vase. Then she turned to face her stepdaughter, and there was a short silence as the two women studied one another.

"Claire – there's a lot I want to say to you. I wish we had more time."

"There'll be time," Claire pointed out, "when I come home."

"I wish you hadn't arranged to go and stay with your aunts."

"It's only for ten days."

"They asked you because they felt that your father and I ought to have some time alone, and because I refused to go on a honeymoon. The very word is absurd, at your father's age and mine. But you needn't have gone away. You've spent too much of your life with old people. Don't let them persuade you to stay on. Come home as soon as you can and let's talk about your own wedding."

"If and when," Claire said quietly.

Her stepmother hesitated.

"I would have said something to you earlier, Claire, but I felt I ought to wait until we were related – until I had some sort of standing. Well, now I have, so here goes: Is there anything wrong between you and Grant?"

Claire answered unhesitatingly.

"In the way you mean – no."

"That takes something off my mind, but not everything. Your father thinks there must be something wrong with the Will."

"There isn't. But . . ."

19

"But?"

"They're waiting for you downstairs."

"Let them wait. You're the first daughter I ever had or ever will have and I've been worried about you. If the Will is valid, why this long delay in marrying?"

Claire, to her own surprise, felt tears pricking her eyes. She forced them back; make-up was make-up, and there was enough speculation downstairs as it was.

"You're sure," her stepmother said, watching her with a worried frown, "that there's nothing wrong?"

"The Will was wrong. Not legally, but morally. There had been an earlier one in which there were gifts and legacies; Grant's mother had told them all quite openly what she was leaving them. And then, quite suddenly one morning, without a word, she left the house and had herself driven to her lawyer's. When she told him that she was going to change her Will, he begged her to stop and reconsider. Her answer was to get up and go to the only other lawyer in Spenders, and get him to do it. He didn't like it, but he couldn't stop her. It was drawn up, and signed, and witnessed – everything."

"They had no idea why?"

"None. The only thing she said to both the lawyers was that they – whoever They were – were all in it. 'They're all in it, all of them' she kept repeating – she was in a terrible rage. It was probably rage that made her miss her footing as she came out of the room. She caught her heel at the top of the stairs and went crashing down to the bottom. When the lawyer and his clerk got to her, she was dead."

"And these people," Mrs. Marston asked, "these people who are still in the house, were beneficiaries under the old Will?"

"Yes."

"Exactly who's living there?"

"Mrs. Tennant's housekeeper, who's called Mrs. Peel, and who has been working there for over twenty-seven years. And Grant's stepsister. She's a widow with a little boy named Paul. She married Mrs. Tennant's godson, Geoffrey Summerhill, and he and she made their home with Mrs. Tennant and Grant."

"Isn't there a stepbrother?"

"Yes. But he and Mrs. Tennant loathed one another, and there was never any question of his getting anything."

"There was no blood tie, was there?"

"None. Grant was twenty-two when his mother re-married; his stepbrother was about a year older, and the sister, Lotty, was eighteen. Their father died soon after the marriage."

"Was the house his?"

"No. It belonged to Mrs. Tennant – or Mrs. Hewitt, as she was then. Her parents left it to her, and she refused to leave it when she married, so Grant's father went to live there."

"And the second husband too?"

"Yes. She loved the house, and so does . . . so did Grant. When I first met him, that was one of the things that struck me about him – this tremendous affection he had for his home. And that awful Will seems to have . . . he won't go to the house at all. There's no reason to suppose that the people in it aren't prepared to move out – but since the funeral, Grant's refused to go there, refused to discuss the future of the house, refused to ask Lotty or Mrs. Peel to come up to London to discuss their plans, or our plans. And that isn't the worst. The worst is that Grant now says he doesn't want the house. He says he wants to go back to Canada – for good."

Her stepmother considered both the statement and the tone.

"And you think," she said, "that he's . . . running away?"

"What else can you call it?" There was a note of desperation in Claire's voice. "He *loves* that house. I don't know why he does, because when I saw it on the day of the funeral, I thought it was gloomy beyond words and I don't in the least look forward to living in it – but that isn't the point. The point is that no matter how much Grant regretted what his mother had done, he couldn't go further than his offer to make up their losses. When they'd refused, he should have left them to think things over, and then he should have gone down there again and talked things over. But he wouldn't. He's been brooding for months, because he's known Mrs. Peel all his life, and is fond of Lotty and her little boy, and doesn't want to turn them out. And that's where we've stuck – for months. I can't tell you what it feels like to watch a man dodging, evading, putting off, waiting for another man to get him out of his dilemma."

"What other man?"

"His stepbrother. The house comes first in Grant's affections, and his stepbrother next."

"Where is he?"

"In Paris. His mother was French, and he and Lotty lived most of their lives in France. He wasn't at the funeral because he'd had a ski-ing accident. When he was on his feet again, Grant wrote and asked him to come home – and he couldn't, or wouldn't, or didn't. And after that, Grant simply persuaded himself that he liked Canada and would like to go back – for good."

"Leaving the house and the problem?"

"Yes. Letting Lotty and Mrs. Peel work it out. Is that how a man behaves? Is that how I thought my future husband would behave? He's afraid. He's afraid to face the harsh fact that they've got to get out, and that he has got to put them out – and that he has got to come to some practical arrangement about when and how. He owes it to himself, and to me – and also to them, because after all, they've been stuck down there waiting for him to say something, do something. I suppose Lotty Summerhill could have asked him what his plans were – but how can a housekeeper walk out and leave a house, or a gardener walk out and abandon a garden if there's a hope of being kept on by the new owner? And that's all. Downstairs, they're waiting for you, and wondering why Grant and I didn't get married long before you did."

"Couldn't you have married and solved the house problem between you?"

"That's what I hoped – but I couldn't get him to see it

that way. As soon as he heard that his mother was dead, he decided that we would marry quietly and go down to live at Spenders – and then the Will was read, and that plan, and all other plans, came to a full stop. I realize that the Will was a shock to him, but how long are patients allowed to remain under shock? From February to May?"

There was a pause.

"When you come home," her stepmother said, "you and I and Grant are going to talk this over. Your aunts aren't going to be much help."

There was no need, Claire noted, to add that her father wouldn't be much help either.

They walked together to the lift.

"It's perhaps a pity," Mrs. Marston said, "that Grant's stepbrother didn't come home and see about getting possession of the house."

"I'd like Grant to see about it, not Richard Tennant."

Her stepmother's hand paused on its way to press the lift button.

"Richard Tennant?" she repeated slowly.

"I've never met him," Claire said. "Do you know the name?"

"Somewhere, recently, I've heard it. But where?"

The lift had been summoned, and had borne them downstairs before she could remember where. And then they were surrounded by a cluster of guests, and the bride and bridegroom drove away and the gloomy forebodings of the hall porter were more than realized: there was no great harvest of tips.

The next hour or so was spent by Claire in helping her stepmother's cousins to complete the business details of the wedding. She had also to drive her aunts to the station; she herself was to dine with Grant before joining them at their flat. Her last task before leaving Gisborough was to go up to her stepmother's room and collect the flowers. She made them into an attractive bouquet and pinned on to it the card she found lying on the desk; then she went down to join Grant, who was waiting to drive her to London.

"Ready?" he asked.

"Yes. Will you go past the hospital? I've got to leave these flowers."

He drove her there and left the engine running while he took the flowers to the door and handed them in.

"Where," asked Claire on his return, "are we dining?"

"I'd like to go up to my rooms first and get out of these clothes. After that, perhaps Soho."

She waited in his small and dim sitting-room, and thought that it was almost as depressing as the house at Spenders. He had lived all his life at home; only on his return from Canada had he taken rooms in town in order to see as much of her as possible and avoid the nightly journey down to Spenders.

A letter dropped into the letter-box and she took it out and gave it to Grant when he emerged from his bedroom. He looked at it, and she saw his expression change.

"Richard," he said.

He did not open it until he had poured a drink for

25

Claire and for himself. He read it through quickly, standing by the window, and then he put it into his pocket without comment. Claire raised her glass.

"To weddings," she said.

She saw him flush, and regretted her words and regretted even more the faintly sarcastic tone in which they had been uttered. He spoke after a short, thoughtful pause.

"You've been very patient," he said.

"Yes," she agreed. "But some things are worth waiting for."

Any other man, she reflected, would have shown his appreciation of this sentiment in a warm, almost too warm manner. But Grant merely gave her a slow, grateful smile.

Sometimes, she realized, you got just what you asked for. She had asked for a man whose passions were under some kind of control – and here he was. There was no danger, when they were alone, of his sweeping her into a fierce embrace and making the most of the moment. There was no danger, full stop. Her somewhat limited experience of men had led her to the belief that you had to choose between the placid and the passionate, and she couldn't complain if her preference had been taken too literally. What had become of the man who had written the long, longing, moving letters from Canada, she had no idea.

He took her to a quiet, famous restaurant in Soho, and while they waited for the food they had ordered, they spoke of the wedding.

"Your father," he said, "is a wonderful man."

"You mean that he looked handsome and happy and at

26

ease, and made people forget he was an elderly bridegroom?"

"That — and other things. I've sometimes wondered
if—"

" – if he wasn't really as strong as a horse?"

She saw his look of surprise, and realized that the irrita-
tion building up within her was finding voice.

"That's putting it rather strongly," he said. "I was going
to say that I sometimes wondered if he'd outgrown his
early disorders."

"Whatever they were. I suppose he's like one of those
old ships that can sail in calm waters but couldn't weather a
storm. How much he can stand, nobody's ever cared or
dared to find out. He was a delicate baby, and they worried
about his health. His parents worried and then his sisters
worried and then my mother worried. I don't think my
stepmother'll worry; she'll just apply a professional touch.
She – are you listening?"

"No." His voice was husky. "Claire, you're so lovely.
I..."

It was, she knew, no use waiting for the completion of
the sentence. At no time talkative, under stress of emotion
he became dumb. He resorted, now, to fumbling with the
knives and forks, and she took them gently from him.

"You were saying?"

"I said you were lovely. I thought so all through the
wedding today. And at the wedding, I realized for the
first time that people were talking – talking about us, I

mean. That gave me a shock. Perhaps you didn't notice the way they were looking at us."

"Yes. I noticed."

"Well, I'm sorry. I hadn't looked at it from that point of view before. From your point of view. I'd been seeing it as my own problem. But it won't" – he raised his eyes and looked at her across the table, and she saw for the first time since his mother's death something of life, something of animation in them – "it won't be a problem much longer."

"Why not?"

"Richard's coming home."

She said nothing for some moments; it was safer to say nothing.

"I don't," she said at last, "see quite how that disposes of your problem."

He did not notice the coolness in her voice, but she noted that he – who had been unable, before taking her down to his home, to describe it adequately, who had failed to give her the smallest idea of what his mother was like, or Lotty Summerhill or Mrs. Peel – was now, on the subject of Richard Tennant, growing lyrical.

"He's been asked to join the London branch of his firm. He doesn't say whether he's going to accept the offer or not, but he's coming over to England to talk about it. I'm glad you're going to meet at last, you and Richard. You'll like him, Claire. He's a good chap. He's tall – taller than I am. And very dark – darker even than Lotty. And clever. I did better than he did at Oxford because I was a good examinee and he wasn't, but he's got a better brain than I have. He looks foreign, and in a way I suppose he's not really English, though you wouldn't know it when he talks. He speaks several languages – speaks them well. He's going to an hotel in London, but he says he'll go down to Spenders on Friday for the week-end. I could get Friday morning off, and you and I could go down there and arrive in time for lunch."

"You could. I couldn't. You've forgotten," she reminded him coldly, "that I'm staying with my aunts."

This time, her tone penetrated his consciousness and he looked across at her with an uneasy frown.

"What's the matter? You sound . . . you don't sound very pleased."

"About meeting Richard? Or at the thought that between Friday and Monday, he's going to clear up all your problems?"

"Look, Claire, if you'll just wait and—"

"If you use the word wait again," she told him in an even tone, "I'll get up and go home. Without you. I've waited for more than three months. I've waited for you to get over your mother's death, and your mother's Will, and I've waited for you to stop brooding and I've waited for you to turn back into the kind of man you were before your mother died. I've waited for you to stop worrying about your own problems and to start worrying about mine. The only thing, the only person I ever thought would hold up our wedding was my father; at first, it didn't look as if I would be able to leave him. But my stepmother appeared,

29

and I was free, and if anybody had told me that months later I'd still be waiting to get married without being able to explain exactly to anybody why I wasn't already married, I would have thought they were crazy. And if anybody had told me that what I was really waiting for was my fiancé's stepbrother, I would have thought they were even crazier. Waiting for you to make up your mind was one thing. Waiting for you while you're waiting for Richard Tennant to make up your mind for you is another. You can go down to Spenders on Friday and you can get there in time for lunch and you can tell me, when you come back, exactly what Richard Tennant has decided – for you and for me. I've waited so long that I can wait for that too."

She stopped. She felt very much better – and, suddenly, very hungry. She gave her undivided attention to her food, pleased at the thought that she had put Grant off his.

"There's no need to go off the handle," he said at last.

"That's what you think," Claire told him. "All that time, while I was waiting for you to make up your mind, it never once occurred to me that you mightn't have a mind of your own to make up. What did you do before Richard Tennant came into your life?"

"You don't understand. I—"

"You asked him to come to England once before, and he didn't come because it probably didn't suit him to come. Now he can fit you in between sessions with his London branch."

"Is there any harm in wanting advice from someone you like, someone who knows the . . . the set-up, who knows

30

me, who knows the house, who knows Mrs. Peel; who's Lotty's brother?'

"Yes, there is – if you can't get on without their advice. The truth is that you don't want him to advise you; you want him to take the whole thing out of your hands and hand it back again nicely wrapped up. Don't you?"

"Yes, I do. I want him to . . . to pull things together."

The simple confession disarmed her. It was the truth, and he was prepared to voice it. Suddenly, her anger left her. She had tried to help him, but she was in one way a stranger – she knew little of his home, of his background, of his relations. He had wanted to take the problem to somebody who would understand more about it than she could.

And abusing him, she realized, would get neither of them anywhere. If he needed a support, the best thing she could do was to prop him up against one. If he couldn't find his way out of this impasse without guidance from Richard Tennant, the best thing for everybody would be to get the two of them together with as little delay as possible. If Richard Tennant could fix the date of her wedding, let him fix it.

Grant was watching her, his face drawn with anxiety.

"I know it means taking you away from your aunts – but it's only for a week-end. Please Claire. Friday to Monday. Will you come?"

There was a pause before she spoke.

"Yes, I'll come," she said, and did not ask whether three days would be enough for Richard Tennant to pull things together.

CHAPTER TWO

Netta was not pleased to hear that her niece intended to rob her of three days out of a ten-day visit, but as it seemed to mark a further stage in the preparations for the wedding, she could not make too many protests. Ettie was not greatly affected by three days more or less; she loved her niece, but she was living in a happy land in which all her old friends made frequent appearances and took her back to the days when she was young and carefree.

The weather was so perfect that Grant rang up on Friday morning to suggest changing their plan of getting to Spenders in time for lunch; this was picnic weather.

"A picnic!" said Ettie joyfully when Claire asked for sandwiches. "How we used to love picnics!"

"Just a few sandwiches," said Claire. "Ham, perhaps."

"Not sandwiches," Netta ruled. "We never took sandwiches. The best thing is a cold chicken pie."

"There won't be time—"

"I shall go and help in the kitchen," Netta said. "Some sausage rolls, too. And you must take some hard-boiled eggs."

"And some salt," said Ettie. "That little shop a few

doors away sells delicious chicken patties; I shall go now and get some."

"You'll need cheese," Netta said. "Get some Gorgonzola, Ettie, while you're out. And don't attempt to carry the things back by yourself; bring the little boy."

"You're very kind," Claire said, "but honestly, all we need is—"

"If they've got any freshly-made liver *pâte*," Netta called after Ettie, "buy some – but not if it's yesterday's."

In the kitchen, baskets were filled with Ettie's purchases, and with the cook's contributions. There was also a mixed salad, biscuits, large slices of fruit cake, a bottle of wine and a flask of hot coffee.

Grant carried everything to the car without comment, merely exchanging with Claire an indulgent lift of the eyebrows. As they said good-bye to the two old ladies, the sun disappeared; they drove away to a roll of thunder and ate their lunch shut inside the car while torrents of rain streamed down the windows.

"Why did you let them prepare all this stuff just for two people?" Grant asked.

"It isn't a case of letting or not letting. If they get an idea that something's the right thing to do, they do it. This is what they always took on picnics, so this is what we take on picnics."

"I see. What was Aunt Netta's husband like?"

"As far as I can gather, he was handsome, rich, and did everything Netta told him to do. The perfect husband – for Netta."

He laughed, and the sound, nowadays, was so rare that she looked at him in surprise.

"So you can," she said.

"Can what?"

"Laugh."

He arrested her hand on its way with some food to her lips, and leaned over to kiss her.

"I'll make it up to you one day," he promised.

"One day won't be enough. You owe me three good months. Was this picnic," she asked, at another peal of thunder, "your idea?"

"Richard said it would rain. I rang his hotel before I left – he'd just arrived. He sent you his love. You'll like him, Claire."

She could not deny that he had a tonic effect on Grant. It would not greatly matter, she thought, whether she liked or disliked him; if she didn't, she would remind herself that tonics sometimes contained a proportion of poison.

"Why are you so sure I'll like him?" she asked. "Your mother didn't."

"No," he admitted, "she didn't. There was war between them from the very beginning."

"Why?"

"They got on one another's nerves, I suppose. Or perhaps he was at the wrong age when my mother married his father. He was doing a short spell at the London branch of his firm and my mother asked him to treat Spenders as his home. So he did. He didn't live there, as I did; he lived in London, but he had a room at home and he used to come down for week-ends – and every time he came down, he brought a girl. A different girl each time. My mother was . . . well, she was a bit of a Puritan. Strait-laced, if you like. What with the girls, and Richard's insistence on saying embarrassing things out loud . . ."

He paused, staring out at the rain and recalling the past.

"Go on," she prompted.

"Things went wrong from the word Go. He didn't know his way round the house, and he barged into my mother's room by mistake and found her a bit airily attired. It didn't make it any better to stop to explain, as he did, that she wasn't showing anything he hadn't seen before." He smiled. "What with one thing and another, things were too lively."

"What about Lotty?"

"That was quite different. From the beginning, my mother took to her. So much so, that she went to work trying to marry us off. But the thing didn't, as it were, take, and so she did her best to marry off Lotty and my cousin Geoffrey Summerhill. His parents were dead, and he'd spent more time with us than with anyone else, and my mother thought the world of him; as well as being her nephew, he was her godson."

"And that *did* take?"

"Not at first. Then Lotty's father died, and Lotty went over to stay for a time with Richard, who'd gone back to Paris. I don't think she would ever have come back if Geoff hadn't gone over there to see her, and persuaded her to marry him. They were married in Paris, but they didn't tell my mother anything about it until they came home a couple of months later. I expected her to be angry, but she wasn't. They agreed to live with her, and they were there when Geoff died — but by that time, Paul was born and my mother wouldn't dream of letting him out of her sight."

"Could Lotty have afforded to go away? I mean, did she have enough to live on?"

"Yes. Geoff left her a sizeable income." He hesitated. "Not enough, of course, to live as comfortably as she does at Spenders. Besides which it was pretty certain that my mother would take care of all Paul's expenses if she stayed on. So she stayed on."

"And on and on. If Richard goes back to live in France, will she go with him?"

"I don't know. I think she'd like to go back — but with Lotty, you're never sure. She doesn't say much. In a way, it's a pity I didn't take you down to Spenders with me that last week-end. I wish I had."

"I couldn't have gone," Claire pointed out. "The whole idea was for you to go down and break the news of our engagement to your mother."

"Richard came over to meet you. But you weren't there, and he walked straight into a big row with my mother, and left the house and went over to Switzerland. And . . ."

"And the next day, your mother died. Do you ever wonder if the row that Richard had with her had anything to do with her change of Will?"

"The row was routine. He didn't tell me what it was about, but they couldn't meet without clashing."

"Did your news upset her?"

"No. It made her very happy. She wanted me to marry."

The rain had stopped. A gleam of sunshine appeared, and Claire began to pack the remains of the food into the baskets. By the time she had finished, warmth was flooding the car. She leaned back and basked in it, and spoke lazily to Grant.

"Did you want your mother to marry Lotty and Richard's father?"

"I didn't know much about it until it was almost a fact – although they met through me."

"When, and where?"

"Surely I've told you before?"

"No. You may have thought you'd told me – but getting anything out of you takes time and trouble. You're not," she informed him, "by any stretch of the imagination a raconteur. When and where did your mother meet Richard and Lotty's father?"

"In France. I was over there with a group of chaps from Oxford; we were doing a tour of Roman France. Richard and Lotty were driving round Roman France too. We more or less did it together – the fellows I was with, after one look, all fell madly in love with Lotty. I don't know why I didn't; I think I was going through a studious phase."

"And then?"

"Well, that was about all. We all finished up in Paris. I'd persuaded my mother to come over and meet me there. She hated travelling, but she came. Richard's father came up from Poitiers, where they lived, and we all saw a good bit of one another. We weren't at the same hotel, but we were together most of the time. Then we separated, and the next thing wasn't until a couple of months later, when my mother told me that Lotty and Richard Tennant's father was in England, and she'd asked him down to Spenders. It was all very friendly, but it never occurred to me that they'd marry. I suppose it should have done; she wasn't young, and neither was he, but they were both very good-looking. So that was that. He only lived about a year after they were married."

"Did you like him?"

"Yes. Everybody got on well – except Richard and my mother. And Corinne and my mother."

"Corinne?"

"She was an old nurse of Richard and Lotty's – like them, half French. She was about sixty, but she'd had a hard life and looked much more. She and my mother fell out over Lotty. My mother wanted Lotty to marry Geoff Summerhill and stay in England; Corinne wanted Lotty to go back to France. Soon after Lotty's father died, my mother got rid of Corinne. Without her, and without Richard, things were peaceful. This will be the first time Richard has ever been at Spenders without my mother."

"Does Mrs. Peel like him?"

He hesitated.

"It's hard to say. She never liked having him in the house, because she knew it meant trouble. I suppose you've got to remember that my mother wasn't easy to live with at any time. She had a very violent temper. But I think you and she would have got on well together. Or perhaps not. Because she loved Spenders and you . . . you didn't like the house much, did you?"

There were times, she decided, when honesty was not good policy.

"I went to a funeral," she reminded him. "It was snowing. It was foggy."

"Yes. But I suppose when you compare it with your house it might give an impression of being . . . rather sombre."

Claire thought it safer not to pursue the subject. The house at Hallowes stood on a headland and commanded a sweeping view of the sea. Tall trees and a high wall broke the force of the winds from the north, but on the other three sides the wide windows of the house looked out on to water. Beyond the wide terraces and flagged paths was the cliff edge, and below it, a jungle of rock and boulder that tumbled to a golden circle of sand and ringed it round protectively. Access to the little beach from neighbouring bays was difficult and dangerous, so that the Marstons enjoyed the rare privilege of a private beach, or at least a bathing-place free from intrusion. In summer, the lap of water, the gentle rise and splash and seethe among the rocks was like a melody repeated with infinite variations; in winter, the house, solid and secure, met and withstood the rush of winds and remained undisturbed by the roar and fury of the sea. Edwin Marston, averse if not allergic to disturbances within the house, had from babyhood been lulled to sleep by savage storms which would have shattered less accustomed ears.

Inside the house, the walls, the carpets and curtains reflected the light and spaciousness that surrounded it. Nothing in its airy beauty could be compared with the squat, shut-in building at Spenders, but Claire was prepared to believe that being born and brought up in a place might blind one to its shortcomings; there were people – and the late Mrs. Tennant would probably have been numbered among them – who thought that the house at Hallowes was far too exposed, too unsheltered, fit only for coastguards or seamen.

When, during the afternoon, they arrived at Spenders, Claire thought that the house had lost none of its unwelcoming look. The trees round it had turned from brown to green, but their freshness did not extend to the drab building. Spring was to be seen, however, in Mrs. Peel's manner and appearance as she hurried out to greet them. Seen last by Claire in heavy black, today she wore a brown tweed skirt, a shapeless red woollen sweater and a small straw hat with an upturned brim that recalled one of Nelson's sailors. The mixture of the likeable and the ludicrous, which had struck Claire at their first meeting, was now more than confirmed: the huge, barrel-like body was set on a pair of thin, spindly legs; her skirt was tight-fitting, her bosom bobbing and unconfined. She had a large, red, coarse face that could have belonged to a Hogarth figure, but under the ridiculous hat, her sparse grey hair was gathered into a tight, neat, austere bun. Kind blue eyes peered out of the rolls of flesh and fixed themselves on Claire.

"Well, well, well, this is a pleasure!" Her voice was brisk and pleasant. "Come along in, my dears. No; perhaps you'd better take the car round to the garage first, Grant."

He put the suitcases in the hall and bent to kiss her cheek.

"How about meeting Richard at the station?" he asked.

"Richard's driving; he's hired a car. He rang Lotty up at midday and said he'd be here about six."

"Where's Lotty?"

"Out with the dogs. Ronnie Pierce has a pup of sorts he wants to give Paul; she went over to look at it. 'That'll make five', I said to her, but you never know whether she's listening or not. 'Pierre's a gardener, not a menagerie keeper,' I said. While you're down at the garage, Grant, have a word with him. It's been a long time. Oh" – she halted him as he was about to drive away – "I've changed the rooms round; I thought it best."

He had got into the car, and Claire saw his hands tighten on the wheel.

"All the rooms?"

"Not Lotty's; that was too much to undertake. Mine and yours and Richard's. I've made Richard's room into a guest room and that's where I'm putting Claire. I've moved into your old room and I've put Richard into my old one. He won't like it, but for the amount of time he spends here, it won't make much difference. You're in your mother's room; I thought you'd rather."

It was clear to Claire that he would rather, far rather

41

not – but Mrs. Peel had closed the front door and was directing her towards the stairs, snatching up her suitcase as she went.

"Oh no! Give that to me, please!" protested Claire, and was waved on by a huge, authoritative hand.

"Up with you! Do you think a small case like this worries me? If I waited" – she was beginning to pant – "for somebody to come and pick up things for me, I'd wait a very . . . long . . . time. Ah!" She stopped on the landing and gave a long sigh of relief. "Too . . . fat," she gasped, and drew a long breath. "That's it; got my wind. Third door on the right."

They walked up a long corridor carpeted in an unattractive shade of purple; Mrs. Peel opened a door and they went inside.

"There we are." She dropped the suitcase with a thump. "I asked Pierre to light the boiler; the house had got cold."

Claire thought it almost as cold as it had been on her previous visit, but she made no comment.

"Not much view," said Mrs. Peel. "You live by the sea, don't you?"

"Practically on."

"Then you'll probably feel a bit shut-in here. I did when I first came, but I got used to it. I always think the value of a view is a bit exaggerated; it's all very well if you've time to sit down and admire it, but the only time I go to the windows is when I'm shaking rugs. Now" – she looked searchingly round the room – "have I forgotten anything? Yes, flowers. I meant to have a nice little floral welcome for you in here, but my mind doesn't run to fancy touches; I'm strictly brass tacks. Breakfast, lunch, tea and dinner, shopping and taking care of the house; not much time for little flower arrangements."

"You don't surely" — Claire turned to look at her in surprise — "run the house alone?"

"I don't do the actual chores like dusting and sweeping and washing-up; I've got a sort of rota of women who come in and do all that. I cook — and organize. I'm so glad you've come down at last. Our last meeting was hardly a social occasion, and I've been longing to have another look at you. But I knew I wouldn't get it for some time."

"How did you know?" Claire asked.

Mrs. Peel raised shaggy, surprised eyebrows.

"How? My dear, I've known Grant since he was born. On and off until he was five, and since then more or less non-stop. I know him better than his mother ever did. After her funeral, he fled the house — surely you saw?"

"Yes. But—"

" — you hoped he'd get over it, and come back? Well, Grant needs more adjustment time than most people. Things go deep, and he doesn't always know where they've gone, so you have to wait until he finds out. His mother's Will shocked him, and he had to have time to get over it. I didn't mind waiting — why should I? While he was debating, I still had a home and so did Lotty. But it was hard on you. Did you," she asked, "put off your wedding, or did Grant?"

"It wasn't a case of putting it off. It was never really on.

We didn't make any definite date; it was just understood that it would be in or around March. After Mrs. Tennant died, there wasn't very much said about dates; Grant didn't seem to want to—"

" – go into it? You needn't tell me; I know him too well. And wasn't I there, in that room, when that Will was read out? If she could have seen his face then, she would have been sorry, because she loved him. But all her life she did just that: acted without a thought of whether, in getting her own back on somebody she was angry with, she was going to hurt someone who hadn't done her any harm. She always had a terrible temper, all her life; she just lashed out, but sometimes she didn't hit the offending party."

Claire, seated on the bed, spoke in surprise.

"I didn't realize," she said, "that you'd known Grant's mother for so long."

"He didn't tell you?"

"No."

"He isn't much good at painting word pictures, is he? I think he thinks, very often, that he's given out a whole spate of information when he hasn't in fact opened his mouth. He—" She paused. "That was the front door. Will you go down to the drawing-room when you're ready? I want to take Grant to his mother's room; it'll be hard for him the first time."

She hurried out, and Claire unpacked her suitcase and made her way downstairs. In the drawing-room, she stood looking round her at a confusion of furniture, hangings, small statues, large ferns, ornaments, pictures, chairs upholstered in a tight, uncomfortable-looking, bulge-and-button manner, photographs and decorated screens, and reminded herself that taste was very often a mere matter of fashion. This clutter was the Victorian matron's dream of perfection; what was more, many of the hideous objects she was now looking at, having been swept into junk shops, were now being eagerly sought and brought back as collectors' pieces. The only mystery was how the women of that period, with their long, sweeping skirts, could have made their way through these rooms without knocking over the countless hazards that stood in their path.

"I suppose," said Mrs. Peel, coming in, "you think this is all very over-full and ugly. Don't forget that this craze for big, bare spaces is just as extreme. Personally, I prefer this kind of thing because you can see what you've got, by which I mean that you can see what you're worth. Ugly, maybe, but solid. What I don't understand is why – disliking it inside and outside as you do – you didn't talk Grant into selling it. Or perhaps you tried, and he wouldn't."

"I had an idea – a silly idea, I'm beginning to think – that I ought to wait for him to make up his own mind."

"And if he'd decided to live here, you'd have come?"

"This sounds crazy," Claire said slowly, "but I'd honestly never got as far as thinking of myself here. You see, the thing became a . . . a fixation."

Mrs. Peel sat on an inadequate-looking chair and turned her good-humoured face up to Claire's.

"You mean that you waited and waited, and Grant never said a word?"

"Yes."

"Do you want to live here?"

There was a second's pause.

"No," Claire said. "I don't. I think the house is ugly, outside as well as in; I could make changes inside it, but I could never alter that barrack look. When I first saw the place, I thought it looked like a . . . like an institution."

"So did I, but I've spent twenty-seven reasonably happy years here."

"How long did you know Grant's mother?"

"I was at school with her. I – this life history is no doubt fascinating, but it can wait till after tea."

Claire sat on the sofa.

"It isn't-tea-time. Go on."

"As you like. Well, we were at school together, and I don't know why I liked her. She wasn't popular; in fact I seemed to be the only girl who could stomach her. But like her I did, right to the end. She had a cruel tongue, but I'm well-cushioned; hard words bounce right off me. Perhaps one reason I was fond of her was because any treats I ever got in my life, came through her. My parents were badly off; my first glimpse of the life of the rich came when I spent school holidays in this house. I'd never seen anybody spending money before – spending, as opposed to having to squeeze it out for essentials like food and clothing. I used to come here year after year – whenever I was asked, in fact. Later on, I married, and saw another kind of spending – my husband spent all we had in the bank, and then went on spending from sheer habit. When he died, I was thirty-eight years of age and had no profession and nothing to live on. Grant's mother offered me a job, and I took it. She wanted me to be a companion, but I said no, I'd take on the house and run it for her. I didn't think it would be an easy job, and it wasn't, but I'm good at keeping essentials in mind; it gave me shelter and good food, and my own way in my own department. I was useful – I took on the job just about the time when servants discovered that they had rights, and were beginning to demand them. She didn't believe in rights, and so you see in me the sole survivor of a large residential staff. I became more useful than either of us had anticipated. She said if I stayed with her for her lifetime, she'd leave me a comfortable income. We were about the same age, but she had an idea her heart was weak. Well, that's what she promised, and maybe that's what I would have got, if it hadn't been for that letter, whatever it was."

Claire stared at her.

"Letter?"

"Didn't Grant mention it to you?"

"No. He wouldn't talk about his mother at all. If he did, it was only to say that she must have gone out of her mind that last day. He certainly didn't mention a letter."

"Well, he'll tell you about it; he's on his way downstairs." Mrs. Peel got up and went to the door. "You'll hear a bell ringing soon – will you go to the dining-room? I've

47

put tea in there; it saves trundling all the things all the way to the drawing-room."

She went out, Grant having to retreat in order to allow her the full width of the door. He came in and stood looking round him, and Claire waited for him to speak.

"I've never thought of it as ugly before," he said slowly, "but of course it is. But when you've known something all your life – isn't there a phrase about the mellowing effect of old associations?"

"I never had any old associations," Claire pointed out. "Every two or three years, our house was more or less renewed. If my father had ever had a profession, I suppose it would have been interior decorating. He directed it all from his arm-chair."

"Mrs. Peel seems to have made a complete change-over upstairs," Grant said. "Richard won't like being turned out of his room. What's she been talking to you about?"

"She mentioned a letter," Claire said, and at once regretted the words. At the sight of Grant's change of expression, she went swiftly forward and put her arms round him.

"Darling, I'm sorry. I didn't mean to talk about the Will."

He held her tightly; his clasp, as always, seemed to her not that of a lover, but of someone seeking strength and reassurance.

"Let's forget it, Claire."

"Anything you want to do," she said, "will be all right."

"Even if" – he hesitated – "even if I decide not to keep the house?"

"I don't mind what you do just so long as you do it for the right reasons, Grant. I don't like the house, but I'd rather live in it than watch you giving it up just because you can't bring yourself to turn Mrs. Peel and Lotty out of it. If you love it and if you want it, you ought to claim it – without waiting for any assistance from Richard."

The sound of the bell made it unnecessary for him to reply; they went into the dining-room, to find an ample tea laid at one end of the vast table.

"Richard," Mrs. Peel said, as they entered the room, "is going to be later than he expected."

"Did he ring up himself?" Grant asked. "I would have liked to—"

"The car firm gave the message. Bit of delay about the papers, they said – but with Richard, you never know. He might have found a girl who wanted to go to a night-club."

Busy at the head of the table with teapot and kettle, she had spoken without thought, and in her tone Claire heard strong dislike, and saw Grant frown. She broke the pause that followed by explaining to Mrs. Peel that after the picnic provided by her aunts, it was impossible for Grant or herself to attempt to eat anything more.

"I got it ready in case Lotty brought Ronnie Pierce over," Mrs. Peel explained. "He eats like one of his own horses."

"Who's Ronnie?" Claire asked.

"*Grant!*" Mrs. Peel's voice was high with surprise. "Do you mean to say Claire doesn't even know that? Good heavens, haven't you told her *anything* about us all?"

There was expostulation, exasperation in the words, but nothing could disguise the underlying affection. She had spoken frankly of his failings, but it was clear that she regarded them with maternal indulgence. This love for Grant, Claire realized, did much to explain her patience with his mother and her long years of service in this house.

"Ronnie," she was explaining, "is Ronnie Pierce, who's thirty-four or five, very rich, single, and madly in love with Lotty. That's who Ronnie is. His farm's worth seeing: all white paint and immaculate. Not a speck on anything – not even the hens. What's called a model farm. Ronnie's what they call a gentleman farmer. I don't know how much other gentlemen farmers know about their business, but all Ronnie knows is that a cow's got a tail at one end. I didn't wait tea for them because I wouldn't dream of keeping a meal back for anybody as unpredictable as Lotty. Claire, you musn't expect much of a dinner tonight. I cook plain, not fancy."

"I could help," Claire offered.

"No, thank you. I don't like people round me when I'm working. You can help me out with the tea things, but there's no washing-up; the women see to all that. I'll take you round the house, if you like – unless you'd rather take her, Grant."

"I'd like to go out and see Pierre," Grant said.

When he had gone into the garden, Claire looked across at Mrs. Peel.

"You sounded just now," she said, "as if you disliked Richard. Do you?"

"I didn't know it actually *sounded* – but no, I don't like him. Or perhaps I've never stopped to worry about like or dislike; all I know is that I'm happier when he isn't here. He's a trouble maker. He won't leave well alone. He drags out things that would be better undragged, long-buried bones, and rattles them at you. He says he likes to let in the light, and I could never make him understand that some things can't stand light. He says unforgivable things in a commonplace, how-d'you-do tone and changes the subject before you've had time to believe you really heard them. He gets you up to boiling point and then – flick – he turns off the gas and leaves you simmering."

"Grant likes him."

"Grant loves him. One reason for that, of course, is that Richard says a lot of the things that Grant would like to say himself, but can't. Right from the beginning, those two got on; it was one of the things Grant's mother could never bully him out of. She thought Richard's influence was bad, but she could never make Grant see it. I don't know what you'll make of him." She glanced at her watch. "I've got time to take you on a quick look round the house, if you'd like to come.'

They wheeled the loaded wagon into the kitchen – a very large, bare, stone-floored room which was nevertheless, Claire noticed, warmer than any other part of the house. Mrs. Peel pointed to the source of the warmth – an old-fashioned range.

"I couldn't get the hang of it when I first came," she said. "But now I wouldn't be without it. Let's go upstairs."

She led Claire up to a large room whose windows faced east and south – but the sun which might have brightened it was shut off by trees whose branches almost touched the house.

"Grant didn't like my putting him in here – as you saw. But there was no point in shutting it up. When people die, they die and one has to understand that they won't come back, however much one would like them to. Or not like them to. This room was her bedroom. In there was Grant's father's dressing-room; when he died, she turned it into a bathroom." She looked round slowly. "My word! I've had many a bloodless battle in here. But she couldn't frighten me, although she managed to frighten most other people."

"Did Lotty like her?"

"Like, with Lotty, is a strong word. Lotty was lucky; Mrs. Tennant took to her from the beginning. But in the end, Lotty got thrown out of the Will like everybody else."

"You mentioned a letter. Grant didn't want to talk about it. What was it?"

"It wasn't anything that led us anywhere," the other woman said regretfully. "Dead end. A pity, because I'd give a lot to know just what it was that went wrong with her that morning."

"You think that something *did* go wrong?"

"I don't mean that she went stark, staring mad – although that was my first conclusion, and the conclusion that most people are sticking to. If she did go crazy, it was during that last morning. She'd been all right the night before, and she was all right when I brought her breakfast

52

into this room. She had breakfast about nine; she used to
get up early, but she liked to make her own morning tea.
I always went in sharp at nine with her breakfast tray and
her letters. I used to take the letters out of the box in the
hall and sort them, but I never had the time, even if I'd
had the inclination, to get out a magnifying glass and look
at all the postmarks. Now I wish that's just what I'd done.
I sorted them as usual that morning, just like dealing
cards, and hers – five or six of them – went up on her tray.
I saw her give a quick glance through the letters and I saw
her frown, but that simply meant that young Paul hadn't
written his weekly bulletin; that could make or break
her day. I reminded her that it was Monday, not Tuesday –
meaning that Tuesday was the day his letters came. She . . .
I suppose Grant told you how she doted on young Paul?"

"Yes."

"She thought the world of his father, Geoffrey Summerhill. Geoff was her godson, and he and Lotty lived here
after they were married. Whenever they talked of going
away, Mrs. Tennant got so upset that they agreed to stay.
Geoff had a comfortable income apart from his salary, but
I think he realized that staying meant a pretty bright future
for young Paul. Never, never, *never* could anybody have
made me believe that Mrs. Tennant would have left Lotty
and Paul out of her Will. Never."

"What happened that morning?" Claire asked.

"I saw her next when I went to the little study downstairs where she used to sit and do her letters and accounts.
Nobody was ever allowed to disturb her there, but at eleven

sharp I used to take her a glass of wine and some biscuits.
Well, I took them. I put them down quietly because it was
never safe to interrupt her if she was busy. I put the tray
at her elbow. She was writing a letter – writing fast, which
was a sign she was angry. On front of her on the desk was
another letter – I got the impression she was answering it,
and I remember thinking to myself: 'Somebody's getting
it.' Then she turned her face to me, and . . . well, it wasn't
pretty, I can assure you. My first thought was that she was
going to say something about the papers – I hadn't been
able to find some papers of Geoff Summerhill's that she'd
wanted the day before, and she'd been very angry. Then I
remembered that I'd given them to her with her letters that
morning, so there was no reason for her to act as she did.
She said – she almost spat: 'Get out!' You can imagine that
I got out – fast. And that'' – she looked round the room as
though unable to believe her own words – ''that was the
last time I saw her alive.''

"Could the papers you gave her have had anything to do
with—"

"– her changing her Will? Nothing whatsoever.'' Mrs.
Peel spoke with conviction. ''They were simply Geoff's
birth and death certificates which she needed in connection
with some stocks she'd bought him long, long ago and
which had fallen due. I couldn't lay my hands on them
until Grant told me I shouldn't be looking among his
mother's papers but among Lotty's – and that's where they
were, buried under the general mess her things are always
in. I put them into an envelope on Mrs. Tennant's tray

with the other letters, but there was nothing in them to upset her. She knew quite well when Geoff was born and when he died."

"When did she go out?"

"About twenty minutes afterwards. I heard her open the window and ring the little handbell that was the summons for Pierre to stop whatever he was doing in the garden and bring round the car. Usually, I used to see her off – see she had everything she wanted, run inside for things she'd forgotten. The last day, I'm sorry to say I didn't. I let her go off alone."

"Was she often—"

" – in those moods? I never saw her quite so angry, but she didn't have a pretty temper. You've got to remember that she was very rich, and not young, and there are very few rich old women – of my acquaintance, anyhow – who haven't gone most of the way towards becoming spoiled. If you get your own way all your life, you end up by resenting anything that gets in the way of what you want."

"If she had written a letter, surely Pierre would have seen her post it?"

"That's what Grant and I thought, at first. When the Will was read and we were all feeling stunned, we tried to look back, think back, to the morning she died. As soon as I remembered the letter, I asked Grant to ask the lawyers if they knew anything about it. They didn't. I looked through the handbag she'd taken with her that morning – no letter. But if she'd posted one, Pierre wouldn't have known, because there was a pillar box at the entrance to the lawyer's office – our lawyer, not the one she went to later. She would have got out, Pierre would have shut the door and gone back to the driving seat, and as she walked into the lawyer's, all she had to do was slip the letter into the box. He certainly didn't see her post anything – but once she was out of the car, he wouldn't wait to see her walking across a yard or two of pavement.''

''Wastepaper basket?''

''I thought of that, too. Nothing. So we had to put it out of our minds – if we could. Grant obviously did, but I wake up sometimes in the middle of the night and wonder about it. It wasn't in her room – I went through it. It wasn't anywhere in the house, as I well know, having turned it completely round since she died. No letter. No letter that could have explained why she acted as she did. All the same, I'm as sure as I'm standing here talking to you that she *did* get a letter, and she *did* write a letter, and that one or both of them was the reason she went out that morning and cut us all off without a shilling's worth of thanks or affection. Somebody said something – why else would she sit rigid with rage in the lawyer's and say, over and over again, that we were 'all in it'? Why? Why?''

Claire could not tell her why, but she found that her mental picture of Mrs. Tennant, hitherto hazy, had become a good deal clearer – and far less attractive.

''Isn't Paul,'' she asked, ''rather young for boarding school?''

''He's a weekly boarder at Grant's old prep school. He could have gone to a day school in Spenders, but getting him ready every day, and at the same time every day, proved a bit of a strain on Lotty. She means well, does Lotty, but you can't cut her out to pattern. She'll be glad to see Richard – she's waited a long time. The worst thing that could have happened was that ski-ing accident of his. It kept him away from the funeral, which meant that he wasn't here when the Will was read. If he had been, he would have seen to it that Grant did something definite, something concrete, something to give us a lead. But he wasn't here, and Grant rushed away as though the house was full of snakes. Lotty settled down to wait for Richard. I settled down to keep the house running – but it was hard to know what to use for money, at first. When no word came from Grant, I took to sending him the bills I thought he should pay. They didn't include the bills for Lotty's keep, or mine. He must have told you that he offered us all . . . well, I suppose you could call it compensation."

"Yes, he told me. You all refused it."

"We did then – but we've had time to think. Nobody wants him to do anything on the scale his mother had promised to do, but it would be nice if old Pierre could be provided for. He's too old to look for another job. It was Lotty's old nurse, Corinne, who got him this job; they were cousins, and she asked Grant's mother to take him on as a gardener. He always got along with Mrs. Tennant – but Corinne didn't. They hated, really hated, one another. They both loved Lotty, and it was over Lotty that they fought. They—" Mrs. Peel stopped abruptly and marched to the door. "Why didn't you tell me how long I'd been talking?

Let's go down. I should have talked and worked at the
same time."

Claire walked downstairs beside her, but as they reached
the hall, Mrs. Peel stared out through the window overlooking the drive and gave an exclamation of annoyance.

"Look at that!"

Claire, looking, saw Lotty Summerhill sauntering slowly
towards the house. Beside her was a tall, very thin man.

"What did she have to bring him back for?" Mrs. Peel
demanded angrily. "Only me to do the cooking here – and
he's got a staff of four. She'll offer him a drink and he'll
hang on looking hopeful, and as there's no clock in Lotty's
stomach, I'll have to give in in the end and ask him to stay
to dinner. You stay and meet them, Claire – I'm going into
the kitchen. But there's one thing I'd like to say first."

She hesitated, and Claire prompted her.

"Well?"

"Be patient with Grant," Mrs. Peel burst out.

"March, April—" Claire began slowly.

"Oh, I know, I know. You've waited a long time – but
don't hold it against him."

"Do I sound as though I did?"

"It doesn't matter how you sound; I'm just trying to say
that a lot of quiet, inoffensive people get put down as
cowards simply because they haven't got the stamina for
rows. Grant never could stand and fight, because he
couldn't bear the ugly things that quarrels did to people –
and by people, I mean of course his mother. You've got a
good man, Claire, and he'll look after you in his own way.

58

If I'd ever had a son, I would have wanted him to be exactly like Grant. I would have taken him just as he was, without any change anywhere – and I hope you'll do the same. You said you loved him; well, so do I. He's been as good as a son to me for nearly thirty years. Be good to him – but don't try to change him, because you'll never succeed. Take him or leave him.''

She did not wait to learn Claire's reactions to this speech. The door leading to the servants' quarters banged behind her and Claire was left staring absently at the two approaching figures.

''I'll take him,'' she said aloud.

CHAPTER THREE

CLAIRE had not taken away, after Mrs. Tennant's funeral, any clear impression of Lotty Summerhill. She remembered her surprise at finding that unpromising details like lank black hair, a long, thin face and large, somewhat expressionless black eyes could and did add up to beauty of a delicate and unusual kind, but she had been unable to make anything of the dreamy, faraway manner.

By the end of dinner, after studying the subject with as much frankness as politeness permitted, the only conclusion she could come to was that this was the first woman she had ever met who could create the illusion of not being there. If you really worked, she had discovered, you could bring her back from the distant place to which she had withdrawn. When she came back, she could talk sensibly and intelligently – but always with the air of a guest hovering on the edge of departure. If she ever married Ronnie Pierce, he would have, Claire thought, a hard time chasing her in and out of the shadows.

Ronnie looked more than willing to make the effort. He was extremely long and lean – so lean that he gave the uncomfortable impression that his clothes were hung on to bare bones. He moved, spoke and, Claire discovered, thought slowly; while he was deciding what to say, he rose on his toes and then let his heels fall again in a slow, rhythmic manner; if he was seated, he made a minute examination of his hands or his shoes or – in the most absent and unseeing way – of his companion.

Claire, going downstairs before dinner, had found him in the drawing-room; she had concluded that Mrs. Peel's desire to get rid of him had proved less strong than his desire to stay. She would have liked to withdraw, but could think of no polite way of doing so, and they had exchanged a few words between long pauses. Once, desperate, he had offered to go and look for Grant.

"He's changing," Claire said. "He was grubbing about in the garden with Pierre just before you and Lotty came in."

"Lotty . . ." He liked to hear the name. "You met her before, at the funeral, didn't you?"

"Yes."

"She's . . . I mean, don't you think . . ."

"She's lovely," Claire said.

He went pink with gratitude.

"Oh, *yes!*" he agreed fervently. "So gentle, so . . . well, as you say, lovely." He picked up an ash-tray and fondled it. "I suppose you know, don't you, that I'm . . . well, to be absolutely frank, I'm . . ."

"You're in love with her."

"Oh – *that!*" He waved the ash-tray, brushing aside this

superfluous statement. "*Anybody*, if you follow me, would . . . No, what I meant . . ."

"You want to marry her."

"Yes, that's what I was coming round to say. For years, as a matter of fact. Five years and four months, to be exact. I bought this farm in October, and I met her the following spring, and at first it seemed all right. I mean, apart from the impossibility of believing that she ever could . . ." He gave a despairing glance at his shoes. "But what really held everything up was – well, she's dead, I mean to say, and one can't really be frank, but she . . . Do you know, I can't help telling you this; I've never told anybody, but you look so kind, one might say sympathetic – she, Mrs. Tennant, went so far as to tell me to . . ." His colour took on an apoplectic tinge – "Would you believe me if I told you that she actually told me to . . . to get off the place?"

"I hope she didn't mean to say it quite so strongly."

"Her actual words were: 'Get off and stay off.' I'd gone to her to tell her I wanted to marry Lotty. There was no question of permission or anything of that kind, but it seemed to me that as I was coming over here day after day, the least I could do was to . . . to . . ."

"Declare your intentions?"

"I suppose you think that's out of date, but that, in fact, is what I did. I didn't expect her to give me any encouragement – who'd want to lose Lotty? – but I certainly didn't expect to be ordered off the place like a tramp."

It was not difficult for Claire to understand Mrs.

Tennant's reluctance to consider this maypole of a man as a suitable husband for Lotty, but she could not understand her dealing so summarily with anybody who looked out at the world with eyes as clear and blue and guileless as Ronnie's. There were worse fates than a scarecrow husband; he loved her deeply, he could give her a good home and a substantial income. Fatten him up, Claire thought, her liking for him growing moment by moment, and he'd be quite a figure of a man – he had height and a certain shy dignity.

"You know" – he was looking at Claire with an expression compounded of admiration and gratitude – "you really are, if I may say so, a person one is able, as it were, to confide in. I hope I'm not giving you the idea that I expected Mrs. Tennant to – well, naturally she wanted Lotty and Paul to go on staying with her; you can understand that, can't you? And I could see that perhaps if Lotty wanted to marry again, there were men who were more . . . But looks aren't everything, and I felt I could look after her and make her comfortable. Lotty was very kind, but if you're told by the owner of a place to get off it and stay off it, what are you to do? It wasn't as though Lotty liked me enough to – well, to come in on my side. Not then. It's only lately, since Mrs. Tennant died, that I've been coming over here again. I've never been able to find out what Grant thought about me, but I don't think he'd put anything in the way. I'm not so sure about Richard, though."

"Why shouldn't he want Lotty to marry you?"

"There was some talk of her going back to France with

him. She certainly seems to me to be waiting to see what he's going to do. I know she likes France better than England – seems odd, doesn't it? – but I understand that Richard may be coming over to the London branch of his firm."

Everybody, Claire noted, was waiting for Richard. For a man who had spent so little time in this house, he seemed to have an undue amount of influence over its occupants.

"He doesn't," she ventured, "sound like Lotty."

"Who, *Richard*?" Ronnie spoke in horror. "Good Lord, chalk and cheese!"

It sounded almost as informative as one of Grant's descriptions. But Grant had come in, and had gone to the cabinet in which drinks were kept, and there had been no more talk of love or Lotty. And now they were all in the drawing-room, and Mrs. Peel was collecting their empty coffee cups and putting them on to a tray.

"No, thank you," she said, to offers of assistance. "Lotty can finish showing Claire over the house – and Grant, you'll find some of Ronnie's egg and butter and milk bills on the desk in the study; I added them up just before dinner and it seems to me time they were paid."

"Oh, but—" protested Ronnie.

"Come along," broke in Grant. "I've let things like that slide far too long."

Since nobody could disagree with this statement, it was followed by a slightly awkward pause, but Claire, glancing anxiously at Grant, saw that he was unaware of it. Following Lotty across the hall, she wondered whether he was unusually lacking in perception or whether she herself was growing hyper-sensitive.

"Where," she heard Lotty asking, "do you want to go first?"

"Oh, anywhere," Claire said. It would all be uniformly gloomy, and the view would be either of dripping trees or damp lawn. How a young girl like Lotty could have lived here for so many years . . .

"What," she asked impulsively, "do you find to *do* here?"

"You mean it seems rather dull?"

"Well, isn't it?"

"In a way," Lotty agreed. "But I'm . . . well, it suits me, I suppose. I don't like some of the things that people call fun: I don't dance very well and I can't bear crowded rooms or a lot of people at once. I like to read and . . . well, I suppose dream. And I paint a lot."

"What exactly do you paint?"

"Would you like to see?"

"I'd love to."

"This way. I'm on the ground floor," Lotty explained, leading Claire down a long corridor and opening a door at the end. "My rooms are in a sort of wing. Grant's mother felt that Paul could make a lot of noise here without disturbing her."

Claire found herself in a child's bedroom, gay with colour – a startling contrast to the dullness they had left behind. Without pausing, Lotty walked through the room and opened another door.

"Mine," she said.

Claire was too surprised to comment, for the room was that of a married couple. The bed was large and canopied, and a small alcove held the furnishings of a man's dressing-room. There were even, Claire saw with bewilderment, a man's brushes laid out, a leather collar box, stud cases.

"Grant's mother wanted everything left like that," Lotty explained.

"Did you?"

Lotty considered.

"No," she said at last. "I would have put everything away, or given everything away."

"Then why didn't you?"

"I suppose it was easier not to."

"Did you have to give in to her all the time?"

"Give in? I didn't," Lotty explained, "think of it as giving in. She wanted things sometimes, and got awfully violent if she didn't get them — so if they were things that didn't matter much, I did them. I hate arguments. Grant hates them too. He always . . . gave in."

"Perhaps it was cause and effect."

"What was?"

"Perhaps she got like that because nobody ever opposed her."

"Perhaps." Lotty smiled faintly. "When I met her, it was a little late for her to change."

"Did she bully your father?"

The smile widened.

"My father was like me."

She left it at that, but Claire took it up.

"You mean you're hard to bully, because you soar effortlessly into regions where bullies can't reach you?"

"I never heard it put quite like that," said Lotty, "but I expect you're right."

Claire had a brief vision of the late Mrs. Tennant, on fire with wrath, encountering this cool, insulated young girl. It must have brought down her temperature considerably.

"And this," Lotty said, opening another door, "used to be our sitting-room. I turned it into a studio."

Claire followed her in, looked round, and once again found herself speechless.

They were in a large, lofty room with windows facing both south and east. With difficulty, there could be traced signs that this had been the sitting-room that Lotty had named it; there were two china cabinets, a sofa and chairs, and in an alcove corresponding to that of the dressing-room, a large, littered desk with a window to right and left of it overlooking the garden. And everywhere, lining the walls, propped on tables and chairs and sofa, standing on a large easel, leaving scarcely enough room for anybody to move about, were pictures – pictures painted on wood, the smallest of them large enough to have covered half Claire's bedroom wall at home. There were brushes, rows of jars, innumerable tubes of paint, and a litter of unfinished sketches.

"A studio," said Lotty, "ought to have a north light, I suppose, but I like working in here."

"How long – " began Claire in a dazed voice.

"I've always painted, but just before Grant went to Canada, he said I ought to paint seriously and try to earn some money. Pierre prepared the wood for me. I hadn't realized what fun it would be to do work on a larger scale. But when I had a small local exhibition, nobody bought anything."

Claire was not surprised. She was staring, fascinated, at the pictures as Lotty turned them round.

"Sea," Lotty explained, gazing at an enormous waste of grey-green. "You live near the sea, don't you?"

"Yes," Claire said, and wanted to add that no sea she had ever seen had looked like that.

"Autumn," Lotty said, of several square yards of reddish brown. "And more sea. Mostly, I paint seas."

With deep relief, Claire saw that no comment was expected of her; Lotty had floated away, rearranging the pictures in a manner that made it clear she had forgotten anybody was in the room with her.

"Has Grant," Claire asked, recalling her after a time, "seen them?"

"Grant? Oh yes. When he came down for the week-end, just before his mother died, I showed him what I'd been doing."

Claire would have liked to have heard his and Mrs. Peel's opinions, but when eventually she and Lotty returned to the drawing-room, it was to find Mrs. Peel taking a brisk leave of Ronnie and going up to bed.

"I have to be up early," she explained to Claire, "and

I like my sleep. Grant'll see you up to your room. Lotty, see Ronnie out."

Ronnie, who had clearly been hoping to settle down again on Mrs. Peel's departure, made his reluctant farewells and followed Lotty to the front door. Grant went upstairs with Claire and at the door of her room took her in his arms and laid his cheek on her hair.

"I looked at you across the table at dinner," he murmured, "and I wondered how you could have fallen in love with me. I tried to imagine you married to me . . . Claire, you *do* love me?"

She assured him that she did, but the draughty corridor with its plum-coloured strip of carpet and butter-coloured walls did not seem to her to encourage a tête-à-tête. She shut herself into her room and undressed, but as she got into bed and put out the light, it was not of Grant she was thinking, but of his mother. Her mind revolved round the Will and the letter, and then wandered to Mrs. Peel and Lotty and the seascapes. She thought of Richard Tennant, who did not seem to be in a hurry. She thought of her own – it now seemed to her – inexplicable stupidity in not having urged Grant to get rid of this mausoleum of a house. Nothing would ever persuade her that she could live happily in it; she had been crazy to bring Grant back.

She did not know whether she had slept or not – but suddenly she was wide awake, listening with a thudding heart to sounds outside the window. She heard scraping, and a thud, and the fall of pebbles, and then to her horror saw silhouetted a man's figure.

She jerked herself to a sitting position, but even as she did so, her fear receded. Burglars did, of course, climb through windows, but they didn't sit astride them, swear out loud and lean down to haul in a suitcase. If they did, it would be an empty suitcase to be filled with loot, and not, as now, an obviously heavy one.

She put out a hand and snapped on the light, and the low series of imprecations ended on an exclamation of surprise.

"Good Lord!"

For some moments the man stayed where he was, taking in the room with a leisurely gaze.

"Somebody," he remarked casually at last, swinging his leg into the room and standing up to brush his clothes, "has been sleeping in *my* bed."

"I'm sorry. Mrs. Peel said you'd been moved," Claire told him. "That is, if you're Richard."

"I am. The bed," he went on, still intent on his study of the room, "should have been left where it was – against that wall. It looked better as a man's room. And you" – his glance rested on her; absently, he picked up a woollen jacket that lay on a chair, and threw it across to her – "you're of course Claire. How's Grant? No, don't answer that; I'll find out how Grant is when I see him. Mrs. Peel must be glad to have him down here at last." He sat on the end of the bed. "Why didn't he come down before?"

"He didn't want to."

"I can understand that – but it's been a long time. I've been waiting for an invitation to your wedding – I've brushed my best man's attire every day for months. I was chosen, but not called."

There was a pause. She found that his complete lack of self-consciousness had communicated itself to her, leaving her free to make a frank study of him. He came to her assistance.

"Six feet two, very dark, owing to French blood on mother's side. Lean and in good shape except for slightly damaged ankle caused by recent ski accident. Not handsome, but not repulsive. I.Q. a bit above average, probably to make up for his sister's, which is a bit below. Disposition tricky; character . . . well, it depends where you go for a reference. If you'd asked the late lamented – when I say lamented, I'm not, of course, speaking personally – she would have told you I was half Borgia and half Machiavelli. Mind if I smoke?"

"I don't mind the smoke, but I'd rather you didn't settle down for a cosy chat at this time of night."

"Morning. One-thirty. The car papers held me up, and I decided to have dinner in town. Then I ran into a girl I knew, and we did a show. Then I made my secret entrance. That was the reason I chose this room; it was the only window she couldn't keep an eye on."

"If you're talking about Grant's mother—"

"Who else would be interested in my nocturnal comings and goings? I used to try to persuade Grant to join me, but by the time he and I became acquainted, virtue had taken a strong hold on him. Besides which, his window was bang next door to his mother's. Death," he ended lightly, "has relieved you of a very heavy burden."

"She's dead," Claire reminded him, and saw him shrug — the first reminder of a French strain.

"I voiced my opinion of her, loudly and clearly, when she was alive," he pointed out. "What's more, I voiced it to her."

"You must have made things very easy for your father." He considered this.

"In a way," he acknowledged, "I suppose I didn't. But I spent as little time here as I could and I don't think it was entirely my fault that his wife couldn't bear the sight of me." He paused. "Grant said something in his letter that surprised me — which was that you wanted to keep this house. Do you?"

"No."

"Then—"

"I didn't think the real point was whether I wanted it or not. I felt he ought to make his own mind up."

"It seems a pity," he commented, "not to have taken the opportunity of getting him right away from it. Does he talk about his mother at all?"

"He doesn't like talking about anything that reminds him of what she did — but he doesn't believe she meant it to be her last Will."

"Well, that's my opinion, too," he said. "I don't think she meant it to be as final as it proved to be. She was a woman who'd be capable, in certain moods, of wiping everybody except Grant out of her will and coming back and telling them – just to see their faces. I don't think she meant that to be her last Will and Testament – but it was. It shook me, I can tell you, to realize that at the exact moment she went hurtling down those stairs, I went crashing down the ski slope. I'm not given to flights of fancy, but I'm a first-class performer on skis and I shall never understand how I came down so hard. I wouldn't like to feel that when she felt herself going, she tried to take me too."

"Did you hate one another," she asked, "as much as that?"

"Big word, hate," he commented. "Possibly she hated me. I didn't hate her. At least, I don't think so. I used to forget her completely until I came into this house; arriving, I'd tell myself that this time, I was going to exercise a saint's patience and self-control. Next thing, she'd rasped my nerves like somebody's nails going across a tablecloth – and we were at it. But not seriously until my father died."

"You needn't have come back after he died, need you?"

"Haven't you forgotten Lotty?"

"She was married – widowed; she chose to live here."

"Lotty," he said, "doesn't choose. Lotty has to be chosen for. And that was where the late Mrs. Tennant and I first fell out. I came here for the first time after my father's marriage to her, to find her trying to team up Lotty and Grant. I don't have to tell you that tying those two up would have been a disaster of what's called the first magnitude. So I stopped it."

"Why?"

73

"I've told you why: because each of them needed, needs, firm underpinning. Married to Grant, Lotty would never have got away."

"But she didn't go away when she married Geoffrey Summerhill."

"Geoff would have taken her away if it hadn't been for the fact that – to everybody's surprise – his godmother took a strong fancy to young Paul. That meant – Geoff thought – a rosy future for a small boy; far rosier than Geoff could have provided. Geoff stayed – but he never gave in to his godmother, as Grant gave in. If she'd gone too far, he would have taken Lotty and Paul away – so she didn't go too far."

"You were here that last week-end," Claire said slowly. "You—"

"Correction: I was here for exactly fourteen hours. I came late on Saturday night. I saw Mrs. Tennant just after breakfast on Sunday morning, had a blazing row, walked out, caught a plane and was ski-ing the next day."

"Would the row have had anything—"

"No. We fell out, as we always did, over Lotty. She told me with the utmost satisfaction that she'd ordered Ronnie Pierce off the place. Then she said that she intended to leave Lotty and Paul a half-share in the house. I told her she could keep the whole of the house, and that if she didn't remove the ban on Ronnie Pierce, I'd take Lotty and young Paul back to Paris with me. And so I would have done; it was clear she'd made up her mind to keep Lotty here permanently. So that was the row. I left, and the next news I had was that she was dead."

"Perhaps whoever sent that letter—"

"What letter?"

"Mrs. Peel said that Mrs. Tennant was all right on that last morning – until she'd read her letters. She'll tell you about it."

"You tell me about it."

"At about eleven o'clock, she saw Mrs. Tennant writing a letter – and there was another letter in front of her which Mrs. Peel thought she was answering. She was terribly angry."

"They must have found the letter, or letters, when she was dead."

"They didn't."

Once again he shrugged.

"Theorizing," he said, "doesn't get us anywhere. I'm more interested to know what Grant's going to do."

"You know what he's going to do. He's going to let you decide for him."

She saw his glance resting on her, and realized that it was a penetrating one.

"I never know," he commented slowly after a while, "why men got typed as the strong sex. Every doctor'll tell you that, physically, they're the weaker. But a man, because he's a man, is expected to justify his manhood by acting like Alexander the Great and Hannibal rolled into one. Did you fall in love with Grant? You did. Why? Because he was shy and quiet and gentle, and because any girl of sense

75

would know him for the decent chap that he is. But now you want to turn him into something quite different."

"I don't."

"I'm glad you don't. It sounded to me as though you did." He rose, yawned and stretched. "I suppose you wouldn't have anything to eat and drink up here?"

"No."

"Then I'll go downstairs and see what I can find." He picked up his suitcase. "Why did you put off your wedding for so long?"

"Grant hasn't been in a marrying mood."

"He couldn't have seen you looking as you do now. Well . . . sleep well."

"If nobody else walks in through the window, I might. Good night."

"Good morning. To be exact, one-forty-three. Didn't seem as long as that. See you at breakfast."

The door closed softly behind him, and she took off the jacket and put out the light and lay back in the darkness trying to sort out her impressions. They had all been waiting for him, and he had come – through her window. Mrs. Peel feared his influence, Mrs. Tennant had hated him, Grant loved him, Lotty depended on him. She herself . . .

She would wait and see.

CHAPTER FOUR

BREAKFAST was laid in the dining-room, but Claire found nobody eating, and no sign of food. She stood hesitating for a moment, and Richard Tennant came in cautiously and drew her outside.

"Come and walk for a bit; it's a nice morning – and breakfast will be late. I ate it last night, purely by mistake. Lotty's in bed; I didn't disturb her. Grant was in bed, and I pulled him out – not gently. So let's get out and breathe some good air."

She paused at the front door.

"I ought to go and help Mrs. Peel," she said.

"Don't you go near her; she's not in a sociable mood;" he warned her. "When I left you last night, this morning, I looked for food and found a pork pie. I don't care for pork pies, especially Mrs. Peel's pork pies, but I was hungry. This morning she informed me, not politely, that it was meant for breakfast."

He was leading her uphill; down, he explained, was depressing; up offered a good view. They reached the top and stood looking across a wide stretch of country.

"How far away do you live?" he asked.

"As the crow flies, quite near, but by the time you've meandered through secondary roads from Kent into Sussex, it's almost as quick to go up to London and down again."

"So that's why Grant decided to live in London. How did you meet?"

"At a dance."

"That's what makes dances a perpetual hazard. 'One day, across a crowded room' is right. Your father's an invalid, isn't he?"

"Semi."

The house looked a long way below them. Up here, there was a strong breeze blowing and she sniffed it appreciatively. Her dress billowed and her hair streamed behind her.

"I used to come up here to cool off," he said. "That was in the early days, when I tried to keep my father out of rows. I always find it odd to think that he died here after having lived all his life in beautiful surroundings. But I suppose he was glad to end up in English soil." He turned to look at her. "Do you go for pre-breakfast walks at home?"

"No. Pre-breakfast swims in summer, sometimes. There's a path that takes you straight down to a little beach. I have it entirely to myself."

"Why is that an attraction?"

She laughed.

"It makes all the difference between going up and down in a bathing suit – or not. Besides which . . ."

"Besides which—?"

"I was thinking about friends. I had a lot when I left

78

school, but most of them are married, or working, or abroad. If you don't marry early and make a new set of friends, it seems to me that you get left on a sort of island – all by yourself. It doesn't worry me much; when I marry Grant, I suppose there'll be a new set. I was only answering your question about aloneness. And anyway, since meeting Grant I seem to have grown away from the friends that were still around."

She could understand his urge to come up to the top of this hill and escape from Mrs. Tennant. Though the house was not far below them, and though the outskirts of the town were almost at their feet, there was a sense of isolation on this green height.

"Over there" – he pointed – "is Paul's school. We'll be going to fetch him later on."

"What's he like? I mean, is he like Lotty?"

"Not very much. I can see myself in him a bit – he's got my way of not seeing things coming until they hit him. Like me, he goes along doing – he thinks – no harm to anybody, and then discovers he's given offence all round. Like the pork pie. I wouldn't have eaten it if there hadn't been stacks of other food in sight, but as there was plenty, I ate the pie – *et voilà* – it's *the* pie, the very pie, the particular and prize pie that was meant for our breakfast. I don't think I'm selfish, but I think I'm stupid about other people's points of view; I pursue what seems to me to be a sane and logical course, or I make what seems to me a perfectly natural and sensible remark – and find myself in trouble. As now. I think that's how Paul's going to turn out.

79

Perhaps that's why we get on well together. And also why Paul gets on so well with Ronnie Pierce. Ronnie's a man who hasn't any prickly side; he takes things – and people – as he finds them. He doesn't even bear Mrs. Tennant any grudge for throwing him out." He frowned, and went on speaking after a pause during which he seemed lost in thought. "Lotty refused him last night. She's crazy."

"That's for her to decide, isn't it?" Claire asked.

"Not entirely. That's to say, if she had any specific objections to marrying him, nobody would have any grounds for asking her to think it over. But she likes him. She knows he's there, which is a wonder, when you consider her complete unawareness of most people. Paul likes him, and he's fond of Paul. There's the farm, with lashings of space for Paul's animals and Lotty's pictures; there's Ronnie, who'd love and look after them both."

"If she doesn't want to—"

"Ever since Geoff Summerhill died, she's been nursing this idea of going back to France. What would she do over there? I'll tell you what she'd do: she'd get herself into what she'd call an artistic circle in Paris, and paint worthless pictures and spend her yearly income before the first quarter was over. Lotty and money don't stay long together; Geoff knew it, and that was one of his reasons for staying in a place where there's nothing to spend money on. What she needs is a base, an anchor. You wouldn't think it to look at Ronnie, but he'll make a good anchor."

"It must be the French side of you."

"What must?"

"Arranging a marriage on the basis of security and good sense."

"Perhaps. But in Lotty's case, Ronnie and his farm represent everything she and Paul could want. If she were turning it down for any good reason, I'd have nothing to say – but she's simply marking time in the hope that I'll take her over to France."

"She might meet someone she loved better than Ronnie."

"She might. But you've seen enough of her to know that she lives away off in a dream world of her own – and something tells me there aren't any men in it. I don't think, myself, she'll ever fall – fall really deeply – in love again. One man brought her to life – and died. I wouldn't be canvassing for Ronnie if he were a full-blooded type who'd pester her – but he isn't. But you still think it's a bad idea?"

"I think Lotty must decide."

He rested puzzled eyes on her.

"Must nobody ever make decisions for anybody else?"

She hesitated.

"Once people are grown up . . ."

"But growing up is something quite apart from being over twenty-one," he pointed out. "I know men and women of forty and over who think – and behave – like teenagers."

"I think that what I think," she said hesitantly, "is that advice by itself is in order. You can tell people what you think they ought to do, but you can't go further than that. You have to leave them to do what they decide to do. Anyway, trying to run other people's lives is something I wouldn't like to risk."

81

"If you weren't of that opinion," he pointed out, "you and Grant would have been married by now. You would have arranged to give Mrs. Peel the pension she deserves, and you would have seen to it that Lotty understood that her term of residence was over. After that you would have left her and Ronnie together at every possible opportunity, and my guess is that – faced with packing up and leaving – she'd decide to move across to the farm. You wouldn't be standing on a windy hill talking to me; you'd be down there making a bonfire of all the clutter and junk, and re-furnishing this, or some other house, for yourself and Grant."

She did not answer. She had heard a distant shout; looking down, they saw Grant waving, and they turned and started down the hill, breaking after a while into a run. Richard put out a hand and caught one of hers to steady her, and they reached the bottom breathless and dishevelled.

"That was nice," gasped Claire.

Grant kissed her and put strands of her hair back into place.

"Breakfast," he said.

"I bet she only takes coffee," Richard said.

"Not today. I'm hungry," Claire said, leading the way to the dining-room.

Mrs. Peel greeted them with something less than yesterday's good humour.

"Sorry it's late," she said. "A rat got at the breakfast I'd prepared. You'll find kidneys there, Claire, and good, nourishing bacon. I hope you're going to eat something."

"Isn't Lotty down?" Claire asked.

"Lotty doesn't breakfast, except at week-ends, when Paul's here. The other days, I take her coffee in on a tray; I found it was easier than letting the things hang about until the middle of the morning."

After breakfast, Grant and Richard went round to the garage to see Richard's car, and Claire helped to take the breakfast things to the kitchen. Mrs. Peel seemed abstracted, but when they reached the kitchen, she closed the door and began to speak in a worried voice.

"Claire, I think I ought to tell you . . . I had a talk last night with Grant. I met him on his way to his bedroom, and asked him to come in and chat to me, as I hadn't had a minute with him all day. Well, he came in and I was just going to talk to him about household expenses when he suddenly said he was thinking of giving up the house."

There was a pause.

"Did he," Claire asked, "say it definitely?"

"He said it as definitely as he ever says anything." She picked up a tea towel and twisted it into a tight ball. "If you'd told me that he would ever think of giving up this place, I would have told you you were out of your mind. Have you any idea how much he loved it?"

"Yes."

"It was the one thing – perhaps the only thing – he and his mother had in common: they loved this house and the land round it. And you may think it ugly, but every bit of it is sound; every part of the house, inside and out, has been well – and lovingly – cared for. It'll outlast all your pretty white villas and pseudo cottages. And Grant loved it. And now he talks of giving it up. Had he ever said, or hinted such a thing to you?"

"We never got down to anything that you could call discussion."

Mrs. Peel spoke in a dazed voice.

"To think he's . . . I can't believe it. Grant out of this house, for . . . for good? The Will was wicked, but it did leave him the thing he loved and wanted most – the house. How can he talk of giving it up?"

She pulled out a chair and sat heavily on it, staring unseeingly at the large trestle table.

"I'm a fool," she said at last. "I'm nothing but an old fool, but I did think that I . . . I did hope that he'd . . ." She raised her head and addressed Claire with sudden frankness. "Well, you can see for yourself: it's a big house, and servants aren't easy to find, and I'd run the place for over twenty-seven years and I hoped that he and you would come and live here and ask me to go on running it – for you and for your children, as long as my strength held out. I tried to hint as much to Grant before he left the house after the Will was read, but I don't think he took anything in then. All he did was offer us all whatever we would have got in the previous Will. And then he went away, and I suppose I should have known – knowing Grant as I do – that he'd had a shock and couldn't be expected to sit down and think things out quietly – but . . . but *this!*" She rose and tied on an apron with a resolute air. "Well, I'm not going to brood. What comes, comes. I know he'll provide for me – but that isn't what I wanted. I wanted to stay on here and work for him, for you both, for his children. Oh well . . . Anyway, Lotty'll be all right. She'll marry Ronnie and be well looked after."

Claire thought of saying that Lotty wouldn't, but said nothing; she did not think Richard had wanted her to keep the information to herself, but Mrs. Peel had enough on her mind.

She went out of the kitchen and wandered into the garden. Richard was dragging a long chair into the sun; Grant was walking towards the kitchen gardens, and she joined him. He led her to the shed in which Pierre was working; a small, wizened man with small black eyes and a sullen expression. He took off a black beret, returned Claire's greeting in heavily accented English and waved his hand angrily towards the box he was making.

"For another animal," he said. "We 'ave already a zoo. There is a dog, a bigger dog, a marmoset, a ferret, there are ducks and now I make a cage for a squirrel. This garden is not big enough. If Mr. Pierce has animals to give, he should keep them over there, where there is more room. All the time I make cages, I feed animals, I let them out, I put them in. This is not gardening."

Grant, agreeing that it wasn't, showed Claire the menagerie.

"All Paul's," he said. "But I see Pierre's point."

"And I hear," she said, "that there's no chance of their being taken back to Ronnie's farm."

"Richard told you?"

"Yes."

They walked slowly back to the lawn, and Richard, stretched comfortably on his chair, called to them as they approached.

"Like summer," he said. "You can't have this chair, Claire – it's the only one that fits me. Grant'll get two more."

"One more," Grant said, bringing it and walking away again. "I'm going to do some accounts with Mrs. Peel."

"And I," Richard said, "am going to close my eyes and try to forget Lotty's painting. Did you see them?" he asked Claire.

"Yes. I suppose you told her you didn't like them."

"Wrong. You have to be careful nowadays; you may think you're looking at something a child did when it was in bed getting over the measles, but it's dangerous to say so; you learn it's so-and-so's latest masterpiece. It's cubist, or abstract, or primitive, or symbolic and if you're not burning to hang it on your walls you're hopelessly out of touch. So I didn't tell Lotty to desist. I gave her marks for industry and I've just sent her over to the farm to collect the eggs – and, in my honour, some cream. If Ronnie's as sensible as I think he is, in spite of his misleading appearance and manner, he'll get her into a quiet corner of the dairy and propose again. This time, perhaps with more success."

She glanced at him.

"Just because you advised her to marry him?"

"Just because I made her see that France wasn't the

86

place for her or for Paul. Which reminds me that I said I'd go and fetch him home. Coming?"

"I might."

She was frowning, and he sent her a lazy glance.

"Thinking of—?"

"Lotty," she said. "She's twenty-six. You don't feel it's rather a heavy responsibility, arranging other people's lives in the way you do?"

He ignored the sarcasm in her voice.

"I take that kind of responsibility very lightly. Lotty turned Ronnie down because she'd got her head full of dreams in which the Left Bank figured prominently. I explained that the Left Bank isn't what it was, if it ever was, and I also reminded her that there was a slight – I didn't say how slight – chance of my staying over here. Then I sent her for the eggs."

"She's twenty-six. She can choose for herself."

"You keep saying that. But choosing means thinking of two things, and that's asking twice too much of Lotty. What's more, there are twenty-sixes and twenty-sixes. Take you, for example; twenty-six, cool as they come, with what my father, who hadn't one, used to call a good grip on life. There was never a man," he added musingly, "who knew so much about the theory of life, and so little about its practice. Heredity's a deadly thing, I always think; he passed on to Lotty all the qualities he'd succeeded in hiding, or partially overcoming, during his lifetime. It's odd that Grant's mother should have liked them so much in Lotty and – in the end – so little in him."

"Perhaps they're womanly qualities."

"Of course they are," he agreed readily, "but Mrs. Tennant would never have married a manly man. Don't they say there's only one pair of trousers between man and wife, and whoever puts them on first, keeps them on?"

"If she was as unattractive as you make her out, why did your father marry her?"

"Now that," he said, "has a very simple answer. He fell in love with her. You've seen that portrait of her in the library? Well, it was painted when she was in her twenties, but she'd kept, all those years, a good deal of that beauty. Lovely skin, lovely teeth, even lovely hair – quite white, but soft and pretty. Good figure – by which I mean no figure; lean and straight, beautifully dressed. My father could probably have held out against all that. But what bowled him over was the thing you've got – that fair, clean, fresh, essentially English look. It went straight to his heart, because for nearly twenty years, he'd been missing England and the English. He left them because my mother couldn't stand them. When she died, he went on living abroad because he'd got the habit, and also because Lotty and I, like our mother, wanted to stay abroad. And then, on a lovely day in Paris, he met a still-beautiful Englishwoman who recalled all the things he'd missed. Little as I liked her from the first, I could see her from his point of view; she brought to mind neatly-clipped hedges, trim lawns, the Vicar-to-tea and copies of *Country Life* and the *Sphere* in the drawing-room."

"His first look at this house must have dispelled most of that."

"By the time he came down here, he was committed; to his credit, I think he merely felt that he and she together could make the place lighter and brighter. He learned, of course, that nothing could be changed. The décor remained mustard and donkey-brown; the rooms retained their Victorian clutter. I've always known why he married her; what I never quite worked out was why she married him."

"Could you have been jealous?"

"You mean resentful because I didn't fit into the new set-up? I don't think I ever felt resentful. I did, once or twice, feel frightened."

"Frightened of what?"

"Of this atmosphere. Of her influence."

"She's dead," Claire reminded him. "Can't you forget her? It's over."

"Over?" He turned to stare at her, speaking in a voice of amazement. "Over? Nothing's over. Can you look at Grant and say that it's over? How could you have let him get into the state he's in?"

Claire, fighting back a surge of anger, spoke when she had her voice under control.

"There must be some point," she said, "when even you feel you're going too far."

He looked surprised.

"Angry? There's nothing to be angry about. You love Grant; I'm fond of Grant. He wrote and asked me to come, and—"

" – and you came this time, because it suited you to come."

"I didn't come before because – this'll surprise you – I felt that it was up to you to help him, if he needed help. Not me any more. I came this time not only to settle one or two of my affairs, and Lotty's, but to find out why you and he weren't happily married by now. After five minutes with him after breakfast this morning, I found he was in a . . . in a sort of trough. I asked you how you had let him get into it because it seemed to me that you must, by now, know that he has a strong tendency to brood, and if you're going to marry a fellow, you ought to know how to handle moods that encourage the tendency. If you let him go on glooming, the thing becomes pathological – and so it has. I hadn't said two sentences to him this morning before I realized he had a sick mind. He's always been quiet and self-contained and inside himself, but he was never like this. It's such a hell of a waste. Here he is with a large income, a large house he's fond of, an attractive woman who loves him, and no trouble in the world except a temporary difficulty in smoothing out the rough edges left by his mother's Will."

"Do you think I haven't been trying to get him out of what you call his . . . his trough?"

"Well, now we're back to where we started," he pointed out. "Where we began was at the top of the hill before breakfast, disagreeing about the exact nature of the help you can offer people who need it. I think you've done everything that a nicely-brought-up, sheltered young woman would do to suggest, without seeming too eager, that it's time he snapped out of it and married you and smiled again. Whereas what was needed . . ."

"Well, what?"

"What I keep forgetting, of course, is that you never met his mother. You never knew her blighting influence, never understood what a wonderful fellow Grant must be to have turned out as decent and fine as he is after all those years of . . . of this. It's a pity you couldn't have fixed a wedding date and got him through it; married, he'd have been under one less strain. You would have been there, by night as well as by day, to keep him from brooding. What's more, marriage would have shifted his perspective – made him look into the future instead of peering into the past."

"This morning, didn't he talk to you at all?"

"Only about the car. He seemed keen to keep off personalities, so I gave him a detailed description of its points."

"He's thinking of giving up the house. He told Mrs. Peel last night."

He spoke slowly after a pause.

"Poor old Mrs. Peel; that must have hit her hard. Is that all he said?"

"He didn't seem to have mentioned Canada to her, but I think that's his idea."

"It seems a long way to run. But the house isn't all he's running away from. The whole thing is a mess. Perhaps she's enjoying it, wherever she is."

"Why," she turned to him to ask, "did she say, on that last morning, that they were all in it?"

He sent her an incredulous glance.

"She said that? When?"

"In the lawyer's office. In both the lawyers' offices. It was all she did say, but she said it in a terrible rage and she said it more than once. Didn't anybody tell you?"

"No. Vital details of that kind bypass Lotty. Her letters were about her paintings, and about coming to Paris. One way and another," he said slowly, "you're not having the good time an engaged girl has every right to expect, are you?"

Claire made no reply. They sat in silence, and presently Grant came out of the house with a chair and sat beside Claire.

"Why," Richard asked him, "did you advise Lotty to take up painting seriously?"

"I didn't say quite that."

"You said she ought to go in for it on a larger scale. And that's just what she did. When I saw what she'd done to those rooms of hers, I thought she'd gone crazy – or you'd gone crazy to encourage her."

"If you're going to collect Paul," was all Grant said, "isn't it almost time you set off?"

"Who's coming with me?"

In the end, Lotty, Claire and two dogs went with him. They arrived at the square-built, lawn-surrounded school to find parents' cars keeping up a busy two-way traffic on the drive; those on their way out carried a cargo of small boys in grey flannel suits and red caps. A tall, white-clad Matron stood on the steps with a school list in her hand, marking off the names of those departing, and guarding a small group of those still to be called for. From among these, Claire had no difficulty in distinguishing Lotty's son. Dark as were some of his companions, none had his olive skin, his large black eyes and unmistakably foreign look. The Matron had some difficulty in securing his attention.

"Paul. Paul! Paul Summerhill – your mother has come for you."

Paul, cradling in his arms a small parcel, came with more politeness than eagerness to the car. He gave a hand to his uncle, a cheek to his mother, a hasty handshake to Claire and then, depositing his parcel on the floor of the car, exchanged warm and noisy greetings with the dogs.

"Grieves and Temperley," he informed his mother presently, "aren't going out. Can I bring them home with me?"

"If you want to," Lotty said.

"No, no, no. Thank you," said the Matron, coming down the steps to the car, "but the Headmaster is taking them out to lunch, at their parents' request; I'm afraid they can't accept your kind invitation, Mrs. Summerhill."

"They don't want to go with him," said Paul, with his uncle's frankness.

"Hush, Paul. Go inside," directed the Matron, "and get your cap and your case, and say good-bye to the Headmaster."

Paul went with manifest reluctance, pausing to express to Grieves and Temperley his regret at leaving them.

"So much," said Richard, "for the illusion that children pine for their parents."

Paul, climbing into the back of the car beside his mother, guarded his parcel with care. A more self-possessed little boy, Claire thought, she had never met; he seemed to have struck a balance between his mother's detachment and his uncle's directness. On arrival at the house, he clambered out of the car, still holding his parcel, and allowed Mrs. Peel to kiss him.

"Well, well, well," she said. "Nice to see you. What've you got in there?"

"A bomb," said Paul.

"A . . . a *what*?"

"I made it myself."

"Will you kindly," requested Mrs. Peel, "take it straight to the pond and—"

"It isn't ready to go off yet," Paul said. "I'm going to do it with Pierre."

"No, you're not," Richard said. "You can hand it over to me for safe keeping and disposal. Come on."

Paul, handing it over reluctantly, went in search of his pets and of Pierre. After lunch, he went over to the farm to see Ronnie Pierce, and brought him back to tea; tea over, Richard tested the lawn for dryness, and then organized a game which turned out to be a compromise between cricket and baseball. He directed, Lotty and Mrs. Peel watched, while Paul, Claire, Ronnie and Grant ran.

It was the first violent exercise Claire had ever seen Grant take, and she joined in Richard's opinion of his unfitness.

"Totally out of condition," Richard said, carrying tea things on to the terrace. "Claire, how could you have let him get so rotund?"

"I was waiting for the summer; I was going to make him play tennis on our court, and swim, and climb up and down to the beach."

"No wonder," said Richard coolly, "he's thinking of going to Canada. Paul, bread and butter before cake — didn't anybody ever tell you?"

It seemed to Claire that he was deliberately setting out to make this afternoon — the first social occasion since Mrs. Tennant's death — as gay and as noisy as possible. Something — perhaps Mrs. Peel's occasional lapses into forgetfulness, when she begged them all to be more silent — told her that there had never before been cricket on the lawn, with loud cries and pounding footsteps and yells of encouragement or derision. Watching the group at the tea-table, she saw for the first time the reason for at any rate part of the dead woman's hostility to her stepson. She could not have been expected to forgive the lean, sophisticated, carelessly elegant Richard his ability, however unconscious, to make Grant's slowness appear as stupidity, to make his observations sound like boring platitudes. Neither Mrs. Tennant nor Mrs. Peel, who also loved Grant, could be expected to welcome Richard Tennant to the house.

Sunday was not a restful day. Claire saw it as a succession of swiftly changing scenes: a rather noisy family breakfast followed by a visit from Ronnie, followed by a two-car party to Church, followed by a cold lunch out of doors, followed by a long walk, followed by more cricket. At six-thirty, Grant and Claire drove Paul back to school, and returned to an informal supper served by the drawing-room fire.

The week-end, Claire realized, was almost over, but Grant, who had come down with the intention of talking to Richard, had said nothing to him, nothing more to Claire or to Mrs. Peel. There had been no discussions, no plans. There was time, she knew, before Richard's return to Paris, for many meetings with Grant, but she had a feeling that Grant had made his decision.

She was to remember, afterwards, the extraordinary beauty of the evening, the brightness that drew Grant, chilly as it was, to suggest a walk after supper. He and Claire put on coats and walked back with Ronnie Pierce; leaving him at the farm, they came back almost in silence, her hand clasped lightly in his.

"Do you like Richard?" he asked as they neared the house.

"Yes," she said after consideration. "In a way."

"Is that all the impact he made?"

What other man, she wondered, would waste a night like this, an opportunity like this, discussing another man? They were alone, and the night was beautiful and he loved her – and he was talking, thinking about Richard Tennant.

He left her when they reached the gate; Pierre was out, and he had promised to close the greenhouses. Left alone,

Claire walked towards the house; ahead, she could see Lotty's uncurtained room and, silhouetted against the window, Richard's tall form.

It was not until she was close that she heard Lotty's voice, louder than usual and full of protest.

"I *told* you, Richard! I—"

"My God!" His tone was one of horror and incredulity. "My God, Lotty! You mean you . . . you actually *kept* it?"

"Of course I kept it. Wouldn't *you* have?" Her voice was a wail. "But I've just—"

"If anybody had found it, come across it, read it – good God, have you any idea of what could have happened?"

"I've just *told* you, Richard. I hid it! I—"

Claire, acting purely from instinct, turned and walked swiftly round the side of the house and then stopped, waiting for her heart to stop pounding. Her mind raced with a hundred confused impressions; the words she had heard, without warning, fused with other words, other sentences spoken by Mrs. Peel, leading her to conclusions as wild as they were groundless.

She went slowly on at last, and entered the house by a side door. She walked along the carpeted corridor towards the hall – and as she entered it, stopped abruptly. Almost exactly opposite, in the room that had been Mrs. Tennant's study, she saw Richard at the desk, hurriedly pulling out drawers and searching . . .

She made a sound, a step, and he swung round to face her. They stared at one another for some time – and then he broke the silence.

"Been running?" he asked.

"No."

"Something frighten you?"

"No."

"Then why the pallor and the breathlessness and the look of fear in the eye?"

"Just . . . something I heard."

His face lost some of its colour, but he spoke steadily.

"When – and where?"

"I was passing Lotty's room, and——"

"Was Grant with you?" he broke in abruptly.

"Grant was locking up the greenhouses. I heard Lotty say she had lost something. It wouldn't" – she hesitated, and then plunged to a conclusion – "it wouldn't have been a letter, would it?"

"Lotty," he said, "is always losing things."

"If you look for them, do you usually look in desks for them? I think Lotty lost a letter, and I know that Mrs. Tennant got a letter on the day she died. She——"

"You mustn't," he said, "let your imagination run away with you."

"It needn't run very far. If Lotty hid a letter, Mrs. Tennant could have found it. You know what was in Lotty's letter, so you can tell me whether it had, or hadn't, anything to do with the change of Will."

"Nothing whatsoever," he said.

"Perhaps Grant would think otherwise."

"I don't think you'd be wise," he said, "to say anything to Grant about this."

"You told me," she said slowly, "that Grant had a sick mind. If he has, he got it by worrying week after week, month after month, over the Will his mother made on the day she died. Now you're asking me to—"

"I'm not asking you. I'm simply telling you that Lotty's letter was an entirely private one and had nothing whatsoever to do with Mrs. Tennant's Will and that telling Grant about it would make him worry more, not less."

"If it's a clue—"

"It isn't a clue. It's just a rather unfortunate coincidence. I'm simply looking for a letter which Lotty shouldn't have kept, but did keep, and shouldn't have lost, but did lose. It was very careless – in fact, it was criminally careless, and while I'm here, I shall do my best to find it. I'd rather not be seen looking, because if I am, I shall have to talk about the letter, which I'm not prepared to do. What I can do, and will do, is to give you my word that the two letters can have had nothing to do with one another. If Mrs. Tennant had by any chance found Lotty's letter, it would have been a matter for the two of them, and nothing whatsoever – nothing remotely to do with the other members of the household. I'm not asking you to enter into a conspiracy of secrecy against Grant; if you want to tell him I'm ransacking all the desks in the house, you can – but I'd rather you didn't. He's got enough on his mind. But I can hear him coming; you can stay here and – shall we say? – denounce me, or you can go upstairs as quietly as you came in, and do me the honour of believing what I've just said. Giving me, in other words, the benefit of the doubt."

Something told her, in the tense seconds that followed, that a good deal depended on her action. She knew that Richard was watching her closely, but there was nothing in his expression that gave her any clue to his feelings.

She had heard horror in his voice; she had come upon him searching swiftly, furtively among papers that did not belong to him – but in spite of this, she found herself believing him when he said that the two letters could have no connection with one another. She did not know him, did not fully trust him – but she believed the statement he had made. And now she could stay here and drag Grant back to a contemplation of his mother's last act – or she could take Richard at his word, go upstairs, and say nothing.

The deciding factor, she found at last, was fear – her fear of involvement. She was not built for situations of this kind. She had no desire to become an amateur detective and to pit her wits against people as clever and as deep and – it may be – as devious as Richard Tennant. She had been given a choice of going or staying, but she had no wish to stay.

She turned and went upstairs. At the bend of the staircase she looked back. He was standing still, looking up at her, but she was aware that his mind was no longer on her; he was shut away, deep in thought, his eyes intent and keen and searching.

She did not sleep until the early hours of the morning. She lay staring into the darkness with the realization that, for the first time in her life, she was out of her depth. She had found herself against a dark, thick curtain and she had been afraid to pull it aside, afraid to walk into the unknown territory behind it. Life had flung her a challenge, and she had ignored it.

Or perhaps, she thought, before falling into an uneasy sleep, the challenge had been flung by Richard Tennant – and she had been afraid to accept it.

She did not see him at breakfast; she and Grant and Mrs. Peel had a rather silent meal, and then Grant brought round the car and put in the suitcases. Only then did Lotty and Richard appear.

"You'll ring me up?" Grant said to Richard.

"I'll do more than that," Richard said. "I'll look you up – but not for a day or two. I want to go and see old Corinne."

Something took Claire's mind back to her conversation with her stepmother on the day of the wedding, and she spoke on an impulse.

"She isn't by any chance in Gisborough Hospital, is she?" she asked.

She saw them all look at her in surprise. It was Richard who answered.

"She can't be," he said positively. "I would have heard."

CHAPTER FIVE

SHE had wanted Grant to talk. On the journey up to
London, he talked to some purpose. He had been un-
communicative for some time after leaving Spenders. Then,
in a quiet, conversational tone, he broke the silence.

"I didn't," he said, "say anything to Richard."

"I know."

"There was no need to talk to him. As soon as I got
down to the house with you on Friday, I knew that talking
to him wouldn't make any difference. It was my problem
and I had to solve it. And so," he ended, "I did."

She waited. His eyes were fixed on the road ahead of
them; he was driving fast and steadily, but his hands were
gripping the wheel with a force that whitened his knuckles.

"I've never been much good at facing things," he said.
"I think I knew as soon as that Will was read, that it had
finished things for me. Finished the house for me. I don't
want it. I don't want to own it. I don't want to live in it. I
don't even want to see it any more. It's . . . it's poisoned.
I . . . all I want is to leave it. Leave it to Lotty, or Paul, or
Mrs. Peel or to anybody who wants it."

"And you?"

"To Canada." The quiet words held something she had never heard in his voice before: resolution. He sounded, for the first time in her knowledge of him, like a man who had made up his mind – for good. "To Canada. I liked it, and it suited me. I felt alive and free and . . . entirely different to this man you must have been getting pretty tired of these past few months. I'd like to go there – with you. But I know you're not the easily uprooted type, and so during the week-end, I decided to tell you this and give you time to think it over and make your own decision. I love you. I want to marry you more than I've ever wanted anything in this world – but I want to leave this country."

She had nothing to say. The months of waiting were over. The suspense, indecision, had resolved themselves into this quietly-spoken summary.

She recognized, vaguely, the streets in the neighbourhood of her aunts' flat: they were almost there. He drove round a corner, crossed an intersection, and drew up before the large, old-fashioned block. He did not switch off the engine; he got out and went round to her side of the car and opened the door, and the porter came out and took her suitcase. Grant bent and kissed her.

"You've got a week," he said. He drew off her glove, slipped his ring off her finger and pressed it into her hand, closing the fingers over it. "Don't wear it," he said, "until you've decided. You must be free – free to decide in your own way. When you've decided, tell me. Will you think it over?"

"Yes," she said. "I'll think it over."

And there was nothing, she found, to think about. She would go, since she loved him. Perhaps there was more strength in his decision to give up what he loved, since it had come to him in a way that warred with his sense of justice, than there would have been in an obstinate clinging to old associations.

And in the meantime, there were five more days to be spent with Netta and Ettie. Five strenuous days, for in her absence, the middle of July had become fixed in their minds as the date of her wedding, and they were not to be dissuaded from proceeding with their preparations. A splendid afternoon was spent at the jeweller's choosing a suitable personal present for the bride. Ettie, remembering that Claire had no mother, made elaborate arrangements with a caterer, and Netta was obliged to cancel them. There were heady half-hours in linen departments, surrounded by sets of towels, sets of sheets, sets of exquisite table mats. There were furniture shops to be visited, and cover and curtain materials to be fingered and priced. In between visits to shops, there were lunches at a variety of restaurants. There were also exhibitions to visit.

"Not," Netta said, leading the way out of the Cedric Turnbull exhibition of ceramics, "worth coming out of our way to see."

"You'll have to ask the poor Turnbulls to your wedding, all the same, Claire," said Ettie. "Your father always insisted on including them because he thought it was kind. I never knew why everybody always referred to them as the poor Turnbulls; they were very rich indeed."

"They were killed," Netta said, "during the war."

"Ah, so *that's* why. I shall wear grey and white for the wedding, Netta. I wish I could wear blue, because I used to look so well in it, but I'm too old for it now. I dare say Constance Rees will appear in red as usual."

"Constance Rees," Netta said, "will not appear. At least, I trust not."

"You're not going to tell me that *she's* dead?"

"She died eighteen years ago."

"You're quite mistaken, Netta. You're getting very morbid. She asked us to lunch recently, and gave us Greek food that made you ill. It made her ill too, but she got well again."

"*That* time."

"Well, we must ask her brother; he's very amusing."

"He's dead."

"Is *everybody* dead?" Ettie asked resentfully.

"Nearly everybody. And the invitations are not, in any case, anything to do with you or me," said Netta. "Edwin has a wife, and it's her place to arrange matters of that kind. All we can do is buy a few things for Claire to start her off in her new home."

She paused on the corner of the street to hail a taxi, and Ettie spoke to Claire in an undertone.

"You see how it is, Claire? She forgets. I wanted to warn you. Half the time, she thinks that people are dead. Now she's imagining that your mother has come back to life. I'm afraid she's going to get a shock when she doesn't see her at your wedding."

"I have a stepmother," Claire said, helping her aunts into a taxi.

"That isn't at all the same thing," Ettie said. "You must" – she paused and leaned forward and pointed – "Look, Netta – no, too late; we've gone past. That was Lily Maxwell. Now don't tell me it wasn't."

"It was not," droned Netta, "Lily Maxwell."

"I suppose she's dead, like all the others?"

"She most certainly is."

"Well, I'm sorry to contradict you" – Ettie spoke triumphantly – "but this time you're wrong. There she was, walking along as large as life. And with a flashy-looking man, as usual. Could I mistake her peculiar walk? You used to imitate it once."

"You probably saw her granddaughter. I've heard she's like Lily."

"It's going to be extremely awkward," Ettie said angrily, "if when I greet somebody I know, I have to say: 'Are you *you*, or are you your granddaughter?' You really make unnecessary difficulties, Netta."

Claire was not, on the whole, sorry when her visit came to an end, but she was surprised and touched by her stepmother's prompt and firm reminder of their agreement.

"You said ten days and this is the tenth, Claire," she said over the telephone. "I'll be at the station to meet the five-eight."

She met the train, drove Claire to the house and presented her with an air of triumph to her father. Then she led her to the drawing-room for a talk.

"Now," she said. "What news? You look tired."

"The aunts," Claire explained. "Never a dull moment. Can you tell me whether they've got all that energy because they were born with all the strength that my father didn't have, or are they making up for all the quiet years they spent down here looking after him?"

"Never mind your aunts. I want to hear about you."

"That won't take long." Claire abandoned the sofa and took her favourite window seat. "Nothing happened."

"But didn't you go down there to—"

"We were down there to work something out, and the way Grant worked it out was to take off my engagement ring and give me a week in which to decide whether I'll marry him and go to Canada – or not."

There was a long silence.

"Well," her stepmother reminded her slowly at last, "you wanted him to make a decision."

"I did. And he made it."

"Will you . . . will you go?"

"Yes. What else? You love a man, you get engaged to him, you agree to marry him. If he decides he can do his work better in Canada, all you can do is go there with him. They say it's the country for the young and strong. And anyway, I always liked those pictures of Canadian children dressed like Eskimos."

Her stepmother looked at her. Claire, pale but composed, picked up a magazine, flicked the pages open idly and put it down again. Her eyes, raised to meet Mrs. Marston's, held no expression whatsoever.

"You don't sound as though you enjoyed your week-end," ventured her stepmother.

"Enjoy? It isn't exactly an enjoy-ish house. It was all quite interesting. There was this housekeeper called Mrs. Peel who loves Grant and will break her heart when he goes to Canada. Then there was Lotty, and a neighbouring farmer called Ronnie Pierce. Ronnie asked her to marry him and she said no, but as her hopes of going to live in France have been dashed, perhaps she'll say yes. There was her nice little boy, and some animals, and a gardener. Mrs. Peel doesn't know definitely what's going to happen to her; Grant didn't tell her. On the surface, it was all normal, if a bit gloomy; below the surface, there was . . . something. I'm not over-imaginative, but I felt it. Do I sound hysterical?"

"A little. What was it you felt?"

"Perhaps it was what I saw. What would you say if (a) you heard that people might be able to understand why Mrs. Tennant changed her will if only they could find out something about the letter that upset her so much the morning she died and (b) you overheard two people arguing about a lost letter and (c) you saw a man at somebody else's desk, going through papers that didn't belong to him, looking for what you can only presume is a letter? Wouldn't you be inclined to say that 'b' plus 'c' equalled 'a'?"

"It seems a reasonable theory. Who was arguing, and who was looking?"

"Richard Tennant and his sister were arguing, and Richard Tennant was looking."

"You saw him?"

"Yes."

"Didn't you say anything?"

"Yes, I did. He told me that the letter his sister had lost was nothing to do with the will. And you'll be surprised to know that I believe him. Did you remember where you'd heard his name?"

"Yes, I remembered," said Mrs. Marston.

The tone – quiet but charged with uneasy meaning – sent the colour from Claire's cheeks.

"Where?" she asked. "You thought he had some connection with—"

" – with a patient in the hospital. He has."

"Tell me."

"She's very old," Mrs. Marston said. "She was brought to us at the end of February – she was found lying in the road some distance from the cottage she lives in in Hurston, just outside Gisborough. It's only a small village, but they knew very little about her – she had kept, as they say, herself to herself. The people who found her – tradespeople in the village – thought she was on her way to a public telephone box, but before she got there, she had a stroke. When I first saw her, she was unconscious. As far as we could see, there wasn't much hope for her. She recovered a little, and then showed extraordinary agitation until her handbag was brought to her. There was a little money in it, and a paper with a name on it: Richard Tennant. She was in obvious terror; she clung to the handbag and became dangerously excited when anybody attempted to touch it. It wasn't possible to know for certain whether Richard Tennant was responsible for the terror she showed – but we took no chances. Orders were given that he was in no circumstances to be admitted."

"Who is she?"

"The people who brought her in said that her name was Remington. Miss Remington. That's all they knew; she had, they said, made no friends there and had never talked about herself."

"There's an old nurse . . ."

"Did you say anything about a patient in the hospital?"

"I asked them if they knew anybody there. Richard said he didn't." She paused. "I can see I've been too sheltered. Somebody ought to have kept me in touch. I ought to have known about mothers with violent tempers who make spiteful Wills. Somebody ought to have taught me how to know when people were lying, and what to do when I found a man creeping round looking for a letter. Somebody ought to have shown me how to take a grasp on life, and then I might have been able to decide whether Richard Tennant was harmless – or not. I should have known whether to believe him, or to recognize him for a cheat and a liar. It's hard to believe you can still like a man when you've seen him doing what I saw him do. I don't know for certain that he's not crooked or even dangerous. All I know is that after all these months with Grant, he seemed to me to have the one quality I've looked for in Grant and

110

never found: strength. You could lean on him – if he wasn't a liar and a cheat. You couldn't lean on Grant."

"Claire . . . you mustn't confuse weakness with sickness. Grant could have a sick mind."

"That's what Richard said he had. Mean or tricky or dangerous, you meet, in that house, Richard at every turn. Some of them hate him and some of them like him, but all of them, without exception, depend on him. Grant can talk of giving up the house and going to Canada – but if Richard wanted to keep him here, he could keep him. If I went to Richard now and said: 'Help me to change Grant's mind' he could do it. If he wanted to. Even before he came through my bedroom window that first night, you could feel him in that house, like a pulse, like a drum-beat. Richard, Richard, Richard. And now you tell me that an old woman in hospital mustn't see him because she's frightened. She's—" she stopped and fixed wide, blank eyes on her stepmother. "But . . . but if she's in terror, what's she in terror *of*?"

"Of losing something she had with her," said Mrs. Marston.

"But you said . . . you said she only had a handbag and a little money and a piece of paper."

"She had something else too," Mrs. Marston said quietly.

"Well, what?"

Mrs. Marston hesitated.

"She had a letter," she said slowly at last.

CHAPTER SIX

THE next morning, Richard Tennant called at the house. He arrived unheralded. Mrs. Marston and Claire were standing on the balcony outside Mr. Marston's room, looking at the sunshine and deciding that it was not going to last, when they saw the car coming up the drive.

"Who?" Mrs. Marston asked.

Claire told her.

"Why?" was her stepmother's next question.

"I suppose because Grant sent him — either with a message, or to see how I was getting on."

Mrs. Marston studied the tall figure getting out of the car.

"He doesn't look," she said, "like a man who would go through anybody else's correspondence. But you said you saw him."

"He doesn't look like a man who'd frighten old women. But you said that's what the hospital's expecting him to do. Will you come down with me?"

Mrs. Marston, after a moment's consideration, said that she would follow in a few minutes.

"By which time," she added, "you'll have found out what he wants."

Claire opened the door of the drawing-room and went in. He swung round as she entered, and by a shake of the head refused the offer of a chair.

"This can't, perhaps, be classed as a friendly visit," he said. "I came to find out what you'd done to Grant."

Claire frowned.

"I did exactly as he asked me to," she said. "I took time to consider his proposal to marry him and live permanently in Canada."

He stared at her in silence for a time. Then:

"Look, will you come out and lunch somewhere with me?" he asked. "We can find a roadhouse or something. I've got to talk to you."

"You could talk here," she pointed out.

"No."

"Why not?"

"Because in the first place, this isn't a house anybody could quarrel in."

"If you're asking me to go out solely in order to—"

"I want to try and talk some sense into you, if I can. Not an easy thing to do, especially under your own roof and in these surroundings."

"What's wrong with these surroundings?"

"They're charming. So charming that they disarm."

"Good. Then we'll stay here and talk."

He was about to speak when the door opened to admit Mrs. Marston. Neither she nor Richard, after Claire's brief presentation of him, spoke; the scrutiny they gave one another was frank and keen, but at the end of it, Claire could not have told what the verdict of either had been.

"Richard," she told her stepmother, "wants to argue about Grant, but says this house isn't conducive to quarrelling."

"You're quite right," Mrs. Marston told him. "It isn't. But must you quarrel?"

"I've certain things to say to Claire, and I suggested saying them over lunch. Will you ask her to come out with me?"

Mrs. Marston's calm, sensible eyes rested on him.

"If you promise not to say anything to upset her," she said at last, "perhaps it would be better if you both went out. My husband doesn't receive visitors; he keeps to his own room, and I don't think I'd care to spend the morning acting as referee between you and Claire."

"I didn't know until last night," Richard said, "what a mess she and Grant were in."

"Mess?" came in surprise from Claire.

"I hadn't," Richard went on to her stepmother, "seen him or heard of him. Or heard from him. I imagined that he and Claire were deep in plans for their wedding. Last night, he rang me up – I was down at Spenders – and told me he hadn't seen Claire and was considering going to Canada – which is pure madness."

There was a pause.

"Is it," Mrs. Marston asked tentatively, "anything to do with you?"

"Yes, it is. Partly because I've got an interfering nature and can't bear seeing people making a mess of their lives, and partly because for some years I've adopted, rightly or wrongly, a kind of protective attitude towards Grant. The thing has to be discussed, but what I tried to tell Claire, before you came in, was that this house has an atmosphere – a gentle, feminine, please-lower-your-voices air. I think I tip-toed through the hall. It's a beautiful house, but I'm not in a beautiful mood."

"In that case," Mrs. Marston told Claire, "I think you'd better take him away. Put on a coat – it's going to be cold and wet."

Claire, without speaking, went out of the room and came back wearing a raincoat. They said good-bye to Mrs. Marston, who watched them driving away with an expression on her face that Claire could not interpret.

"Now," Richard said, as they came out into the road. "Where would there be a decent restaurant?"

"Let's go to Brighton," she said. "I'm in a Brighton mood."

"No. Not Brighton. Somewhere quiet."

She directed him, and they drove for some time in silence. He had come to talk of Grant, and she supposed that soon he would begin to talk of him, and she wondered what he would say if she told him that since Grant had left her at her aunt's house on Monday morning, she had scarcely given him a thought. To think of him was to find herself edging once more towards problems, and she felt that there had been problems enough. He had made his decision and so had she, and thinking was an unsettling process. All she had to do was wait. Grant would come back, would put on her ring again, would marry her and take her to Canada.

The restaurant was an old building set in pleasant gardens. The dining-room opened on to a wide terrace, but the cold driving rain that had begun to fall mocked the array of tables and the gay umbrellas. The bar was over-crowded and noisy, and after glancing into its smoke-laden interior, Richard took Claire's arm and directed her to-wards the dining-room. They were given a good table and handed menus as large as fire-screens; Richard, disappear-ing behind his, gave his whole attention to food and later, behind a wine list, to drink. Then he lit a cigarette, put his arms on the table and studied his companion at leisure.

"Don't you ever smoke?" he asked.

"No. I tried it and didn't like it. That wasn't what you brought me out to talk about?"

"Not altogether. It's just part of the process of finding out what sort of woman you are."

"You ought to know by now. The passive type. I could have taken Grant in hand, managed him, pushed him around – instead of which, I didn't do anything. I'm still doing it. He took my ring off and said I wasn't to wear it until I'd decided whether I wanted to go to Canada with him or not, but as it seemed to me that the decision had to be his . . ."

"Didn't you argue with him at all?"

"No, I didn't. I'm sick of arguing. If you're interested,

I'm also sick of Grant's hesitations. It was a relief to hear him saying something definite for a change."

"And just so long as it's definite, you don't mind whether it's right for you both – or wrong?"

"Perhaps," said Claire, "you don't – in spite of the impression I gathered from Mrs. Peel – really know very much about women. Roughly, they divide into two kinds: the kind that like bossing their husbands, and the kind that don't. I'm sorry if I give you the idea that I'm spineless, but Grant seems to like me that way."

"When I first saw you – remember that I was looking at you purely as a suitable wife for Grant – I was very happy, not to say uplifted."

"Thank you."

"You looked a little passionless, but that wasn't my affair; that was for Grant to sort out. You were beautiful, which meant that he must be longing to marry you quickly. You looked intelligent, which I thought meant that you understood what you'd taken on. Next day, I discovered that you didn't – and I also discovered that Grant was sunk in a sort of stupor of misery. I think I hoped, when we talked about him in the garden, that you'd treat me as a sort of one-man advisory bureau. I thought you'd understand that, whether you liked me or not, whether you thought the matter had anything to do with me or not, I was the only person in Grant's life who had ever succeeded in breaking through his protective shell. It had grown round him all his life because he must have known, always – unconsciously, subconsciously – that his mother's good

117

qualities were all skin deep, and that below them – just
below – was a slumbering tiger. He grew up in fear. Not,
of course, fear of physical violence, but fear of scenes, of
un-obvious but implacable opposition; of mean, shifty
tricks to get her own way. Mrs. Peel knew all about it –
especially towards the end, when the mask was slipping.
You reminded me that she was dead, but I have to remind
you that she's still with Grant. He needed support and protection, in her lifetime, and he still needs it. And when you
let Grant send you away, let him make the wrong decisions,
you're not giving it to him. You may tell yourself that
you're just accepting his decision; to me, it looks very much
as though you'd run out on him."

There was a pause; food was laid before them, wine was
brought and tested and approved.

"Eat," he advised. "It's all good, and you'll need your
strength." He looked keenly at her, his fork suspended.
"Perhaps," he said slowly, "what I thought was a lack of
passion was only a lack of pity."

"If you have to pity your husband, what does that make
him?"

Richard frowned.

"You paid for a lion, didn't you?" he said. "And you
couldn't, you wouldn't believe they'd sold you a rabbit.
Roar, damn you, roar, you said to him. And so I sit here
with you, enjoying your beauty, while he pines for you,
waits for you in his airless little flat. You wanted your lion
to go down to his home when his mother died, and deal
adequately with the mess she left. You wouldn't help him

because you were afraid that people would think you were the pushing type. Why, instead of thinking about yourself, didn't you go down with him and – just for a start – send for a taxi and get rid of my sister?"

"Several taxis."

"Quite so. Grant knew how deeply dug in she was; you didn't. He knew something else that you didn't know: that Lotty doesn't do anything until she has to; he knew that getting her out would mean more or less dynamiting her out. He couldn't do it. He didn't want to do it. He's fond of Lotty – as far as anybody can be fond of someone who lives in a separate world. I only saw her come down to earth once, and that was when she fell in love. He died, and she went away again and stayed away."

"Was that letter from him?" she asked. "The one she lost."

"It was."

"Is it so important – an old love-letter?"

"This one was – is."

"You lied about it, didn't you?"

He hesitated.

"Are you side-tracking?" he asked.

"Not really. Everything you've been saying suggests that you think that you and I could have formed a sort of help-Grant club all on our own. If you begin by lying, by being proved a liar . . ."

"Go on," he urged gently. "Go on and say it. People who tell lies are what you've just called them – liars. The word's ugly, the deed's ugly, but if it's a fact you're faced with, you've got to call it what it is. You've been afraid, right from the start, of calling Grant weak. You've made excuses for his hesitations, not out of pity, but because you were afraid of the word vacillating. Why? Grant's not weaker than a million good husbands and fathers. He's not weak physically or intellectually or even morally, except in the sword-and-spear, bow-and-arrow, bluster-and-bravado department. Are you in love with him, Grant, or with someone you saw on television riding a great, big horse who looked just like him? Is weakness a drawback? If you married me, instead of the weak and gentle Grant, could you really stand up to it? Could you? I'm strong in the way you want Grant to be strong, and from the moment I saw you sitting up in bed, all ruffles and lace and white throat and other things we needn't go into, I fell crazily and very strongly in love with you. Married to a man like me, could you stand up to having that maddening, cool marble surface peeled off, chipped off, night after beautiful night? Burnt off? No, marble wouldn't burn. But then, is it marble? Grant must be wondering at this moment. Claire – dear, beautiful, utterly misguided Claire – will you go to him? Will you take him in your smooth arms and let his poor tired, aching head rest on your compassionate breast and give him strength, if you have any strength? Will you? Will you put him out of his misery and marry him and love and cherish him and also lift all his loads on to your shapely shoulders? Will you?"

There was a long, unbroken silence. The waiter brought fruit, coffee, a bill; mechanically, Richard placed money on the plate. It was taken away and they were left with their eyes on one another, still silent.

"Say something," he said abruptly at last.

"Tell me something," she countered. "Why should a woman leave a sheltered home, and peace and safety, unless she can be assured of getting, not giving, support and protection? You talk about strength; you explained that Grant had to learn how to be strong. Perhaps I have to learn, too. You've seen the problem from his point of view; now look at mine. I met and loved Grant. I don't, didn't mind whether he was unduly strong or not, because most ordinary people, leading ordinary lives, have more or less ordinary problems to confront. Barring accidents, barring tragedy, they can get along. But I found that Grant's problems weren't ordinary ones. I found that his mother was violent and revengeful, the house he loved so much was full of secrets. There was a mystery — a letter. You called that a side-track, but it was filling Grant's mind, and Mrs. Peel's. You were asked about it; you've just admitted lying."

"Haven't you ever told a lie? If you haven't, you've missed a lot. Lies are stimulating things; when you tell them, you don't know whether you've pulled it off, or whether you haven't; whether they've been swallowed and you're safe, or not swallowed, leaving you with one more sin added to your original one. You ought to try it — on your own father, perhaps. 'Where have you been, daughter?' 'Nowhere, father.' 'Not out to lunch with a man who told you he loved you?' 'No, father.'"

121

"Why did you lie?"

"Because the letter wasn't your business, or Mrs. Peel's business, or even my business. It was purely Lotty's business. But you overheard our conversation, or part of it, and you saw me looking for the letter, and ever since then you've marked me down as a villain, and you've been going round like that silly little Jane Austen heroine who'd been reading heady melodrama and saw villains every way she looked. What am I to do with you?"

"You could take me home."

He took her home, and Mrs Marston, coming in from the garden, met them on the drive.

"It wasn't," Richard told her, "a success."

"I didn't think it would be," she said with composure. "If you had stopped to ask my advice, I would have told you that Claire is in many ways like her father, and has a way of pretending that troublesome things aren't there. I find it very restful. Will you stay to tea?"

"No, thank you. I've got some things to do – one of them being to visit a place you know well – the hospital at Gisborough."

There was a moment's pause.

"You know somebody there?" Mrs. Marston asked.

"My old nurse. My sister's old nurse. Name of Corinne Remington – half French, like myself. I wondered why I hadn't heard from her for so long, but I assumed my sister was in touch. When Claire asked about an old lady in hospital, I didn't realize, until I talked to Lotty, that it might be Corinne. I looked her up – she lives in a village called Hurston — and found she'd had a stroke and been taken to Gisborough. Is it unethical to tell me how she is?"

"She's much better."

"Good. I'm looking in this evening."

When he had driven away, Claire turned to her stepmother.

"Why didn't you tell him he wouldn't get in?"

"Why didn't you?"

"Did you expect me to?"

"No, I didn't," Mrs. Marston replied. "But in your place, I would have said something, and I would have said it before now."

"To warn him?"

"No. To find out the truth. He looked for a letter, and there's one at the hospital. If he's a liar and a frightener of a defenceless old woman, you ought to know before you go out to a friendly lunch with him."

They turned and walked to the house together.

"Do you," Claire asked, "like him?"

"Like? Liking him is easy; he's got all the charm in the world. But . . ."

"But you wouldn't trust him?"

The answer was long in coming, and Claire became aware that a great deal hung upon it. When it came, it was not a direct answer.

"If I were you," her stepmother said quietly, "I would keep away from him."

CHAPTER SEVEN

KEEPING away was advice which Claire felt would have been more usefully addressed to Richard Tennant, for before the next morning was half spent, his car entered the drive and came to rest behind the large hired Daimler in which Netta and Ettie had arrived for a day's visit to their brother. Claire, engaged in getting the two old ladies out of the car and up the steps, found him taking one on each arm and making slow but stately progress towards the drawing-room, Ettie clearly enjoying making her entry on a strong young man's arm.

"Did I," she asked him, "know your grandfather?"

"I hope you knew both of them," Richard said. "One was French and the other was English."

"Dear me; wasn't that rather confusing?"

"Not very. One just had to remember which language one had to speak, that was all."

"I was always very good at languages," Ettie told him, on their arrival in the drawing-room. "I think I should have taken them up."

The sisters were placed in comfortable chairs; wine and

biscuits were brought in and Richard served the old ladies as though they belonged to him.

"This is very pleasant indeed," Ettie said. "And so nice for poor Claire to be taken out of herself."

"Why should Claire," inquired Netta sharply, "require taking out of herself?"

"That horrid business," Ettie replied, in an aside. "Did you," she asked Claire, "ever discover what became of that young man?"

"He's in London and he and Claire are going to be married soon," said Netta. "I wish you'd keep your wits about you, Ettie. Sometimes I think—"

Nobody knew what she thought, for Mrs. Marston had risen and was waiting to conduct her to her brother's room; Mr. Marston had lately begun to feel that he was unable to cope with both sisters simultaneously. Ettie watched them go with obvious relief, and then settled down for a chat.

"You mustn't misunderstand your aunt Netta," she said to Claire. "It's just that she's beginning to mix up things. Especially when we're in this house. My sister and I," she informed Richard, "were born and brought up here."

"It's a beautiful house," he said.

"Yes. And so prettily got up. My sister Netta, you know, was married from here, I can't tell you exactly how many years ago. They made an extremely handsome couple – he was a soldier or a sailor, I forget which, and there were a great many guests, and two marquees, and I was one of the bridesmaids and we wore blue. I do hope Claire will have pretty bridesmaids – they do make a wedding, I always think. The presents were put into the dining-room and there was a policeman to see that nobody . . . well, touched them. They dressed him up to look like everybody else, and he pretended to be admiring the things. And Claire's father was a little page."

"A page!" Richard echoed in pardonable surprise.

"Yes; he was a good deal younger than we were. Netta was only nineteen; I was a year younger but Claire's father – or perhaps, as he wasn't her father then, I should say my brother – was only two, and looked like an angel. He was dressed as a soldier or a sailor, I forget which. And then Netta went off and everybody said I would be next, but I wasn't; I stayed at home, like Claire, and then Netta's husband died and she came back again. It was very convenient, because she was able, later on, to help me to look after my brother until he married."

"But he," Richard prompted, "wouldn't have married here."

"Oh dear me, no. His wife's home was about fifteen miles away. Not as pretty a setting as Hallowes for a wedding. We drove over there with my brother and then they went on a honeymoon to Corsica – no, that was where Netta went. I think Claire's father went somewhere quite near, on account of his health. Hasn't Claire ever shown you old photographs of her parents?"

"No."

"You must let him see them, Claire. He really was . . . well, you could really have called him a beautiful young

126

man. Spiritual, they used to say. We were a very good-looking family, though perhaps it sounds vain to say so. I was always told that I had a great look of the Queen."

She paused, but nobody asked which Queen.

"Some people," she went on, "called me a flirt, but they were wrong. A flirt is a young woman who makes advances, and I never did anything of the sort. Perhaps Netta was right when she said I encouraged Captain Sayers, but then there was some excuse; he was not only exceedingly handsome and distinguished, but he was a hero."

"V.C.?" Richard suggested respectfully.

"No, it wasn't a war. He dashed out into the road and stopped an omnibus when the horses had bolted. I still have the newspaper account."

There was a pause; Ettie seemed to come back to the present, and remember that she was no longer young and flirtatious, and did not resemble the Queen.

"I've talked far too much," she said. "That's something that happens to you when you grow old – you talk too much because the past seems so much nicer than the present. I wouldn't care to be young today."

"Why not?" Richard asked.

"Because it's almost impossible to get across a road, for one thing. And at concerts, they play music one simply cannot understand. And painting isn't an art any more; it's a hobby. And if you haven't grown up with an understanding of science, you can't follow all the new wonders they keep discovering. When I was young and went to the circus, I used to see the men who were blown out of the cannon, but

I didn't dream that in my lifetime, they'd blow them right round the moon. But *you*," she told them both, "quite rightly like things the way they are. Now run along and enjoy yourselves and don't waste any more time indoors."

Claire hesitated. Something told her that if she did not go out, it would be extremely difficult to make Richard go away. He had assumed a bland, one-of-the-family manner which had clearly been accepted by Netta and Ettie. There was nothing to choose between giving in to high-handed behaviour, and passing yet another long, slow day with her father and her aunts, leaving them together for not too long, arranging their afternoon and amusing them through the interminable interval between tea and an early dinner.

"Come out and lunch with me," she heard Richard saying.

"Yes, go, Claire. Your aunt Netta and I will be perfectly happy talking to your father. Run along."

Claire went, but only in search of her stepmother. She waylaid her on her way back from Mr. Marston's room, and put the problem before her.

"He wants me to go out to lunch. If I don't go, it won't be easy to get rid of him."

"I can see that. But if you'd like me to——"

"No."

"Why not?"

"Because coming up to look for you just now, I had a rather peculiar feeling of . . . freedom. Ever since my mother died, I've had to stay in and look after visitors – especially Netta and Ettie. But now – there's you. I don't have to stay here; I can go out and leave everything – and that includes Father – to you. I'm free." She held out a ringless hand. "See? Even free, for today, from Grant. I'm not trying to say that I've been tied unwillingly to anything – but I have been tied, and today I'm not. It's a good feeling. I don't only feel free, I feel rather reckless. I don't know very much about Richard, but where's the harm in going out with him? Should I go?"

Her stepmother's eyes took in a good deal that Claire had no idea was open to the keen, professional scrutiny.

"Why not?" she said at last. "You haven't any more heavy duties as a daughter, and you haven't yet assumed the duties of a wife; I'd rather you went out feeling free than feeling reckless, but there is nothing to keep you at home today."

Claire went out to the car with Richard, and he drove for a time in silence; they were going towards the coast, but she did not know where, and decided not to ask.

"Your aunts," he said at last, "are rather other-worldly."

"Only one."

"Did you grow up with the ghosts?"

"No. They've been appearing quite recently, since Aunt Ettie's memory began to get shaky. It isn't often she can create the atmosphere she created just now, because Netta pulls her up."

"Pulls her back. I wonder whether I'll sound three hundred years old when I tell my grandchildren little tit-bits of my life history? I suppose so. Will I ask them quaveringly to drive more carefully – in their space ships?

Did the oncoming generation always leave the last one so far behind? Will we – you and I – appear as unreal as Ettie when we're her age?"

"We shall know – when we're her age. I'm glad you liked her."

"Liked? I could sit at her feet, listening, all day." He glanced at her. "Your aunts and your father . . . make it easier to understand you. They account for your air. Did you know that you had an air?"

"I'd hate to think I had."

"I don't mean a proud air. Just an air; just a slight don't-touch look. Tell me," he invited, "about your life."

"You didn't come down today to hear about my life."

"No, but what I've got to say can wait. When I arrived at your house, it seemed urgent and almost desperate; perhaps Ettie put it into better perspective. You were born—?"

"At Hallowes."

"Well, go on."

"A governess until I was eight."

"They still exist?"

"This one did. I called her Miss Wood, but I gathered, I don't quite know how, that she had been married and that it had been a mistake. Then she went away and I went to school. And then Aunt Ettie took me abroad; it was the last time she ever travelled far, and she looked as though she wouldn't survive the Channel crossing, but we were away for eight months and it was wonderful. Except in the evening, when she used to discourage strangers from joining us."

"Don't tell me you encouraged strangers?"

"I longed to encourage some of them. We used to dine out on the most heavenly terraces – not actually in Rome or Paris or Florence or Venice, but little places, little quiet, safe, well-recommended places just outside. After dinner, there might be music or even dancing, but at that stage, Aunt Ettie had to go to bed."

"You couldn't have tucked her up and climbed over your balcony?"

"I could, but it seemed ungrateful. She was giving me such a wonderful trip."

"Couldn't you have gone with someone younger?"

"No."

"Not allowed?"

"I suppose I could have argued and got my own way. My father and my mother weren't tyrants or warders; they were simply out of date, that's all. It's easy to say I should have got away, but they were my parents, and I loved them and leaving home meant leaving for good, because it meant deciding I couldn't lead their life; it meant discarding it and them. Outwardly, on that trip, I was a rather awkward, shy English girl dogged by an ancient relation – but it was the happiest time I ever spent."

"Except after dinner."

"Yes. But that wasn't active rebellion. I couldn't dance in those days, and I was dead tired after doing so much all

131

day, and it wasn't really difficult to see all the gay young couples going off into the night without me."

"Didn't anyone ever try to storm the citadel?"

She laughed.

"Once or twice."

"Who were they?"

"One was a . . . well, does it matter? It wasn't a question of storming; all they had to do was to sit through Aunt Ettie's stories about horse buses. It became a sort of test. When I saw you this morning, carried away into her world, I was grateful to you, because so few people fall under the spell. It *is* a spell. I love them both and I can't bear to see them . . . going."

"How," he asked after a time, "did Grant make the grade?"

"Through his letters from Canada. I liked him before he went, and I loved him when he came back. It was as simple as that."

"Did he talk much about his home?"

"He talked about the house, but not about the people in it. Didn't you, incidentally, come to talk about Grant?"

He drove into a small clearing on the side of the road, switched off the engine and turned to face her.

"Yes, I did," he said, and she saw that he had dropped his light manner. "Mrs. Peel is coming up to London to-morrow – or Grant's going down there – I'm not sure which. Anyway, they're going to meet. He's going to make the house over to her."

It was a shock, and she sat still, absorbing it.

"No comment?" he asked at last.

"It's his house."

"When you marry him, it'll be yours too. He's running out on it, but perhaps his – your – children will want it. It's a valuable property, and it'll go on increasing in value; I don't know whether you know how much land goes with it, but it's plenty. To let Mrs. Peel have it for life is one thing; to hand the thing over entirely is sheer madness. You've got to do something."

"It isn't mine until we're married. We won't be married by tomorrow. Does Mrs. Peel know what he intends to do?"

"Yes. He wrote to her."

"She might refuse."

"Why should she refuse? If Grant were staying in this country, she probably would; she loves him like a son and she wouldn't take his house from him, even if he wasn't going to live in it. But with Grant gone, who's left?"

"Lotty and Paul."

"Lotty's going to marry Ronnie Pierce. And don't ask me if she loves him, because the answer would probably be no, and we'd proceed to a quarrel about my having pushed her into a loveless marriage. Lotty loved once. She fell in love in a way that I don't think she'll fall in love again – but what happier fate could a woman in her position have than being looked after for the rest of her life by a man as decent and as clean and as straight as Ronnie Pierce? What better background could there be for young Paul? He and Ronnie get on, and will continue to get on.

There ought to be more children – there will be more children. Would you rather see her turning Ronnie down and waiting for her next grand passion?"

"She was brought up in France. She wanted to go back there."

"The one thing she needs – don't I know? – is *roots*. We've never had them, Lotty and I. My father was an expatriate and so am I. Lotty would like to be, but there's nothing for her to go back to and she'll be safe all her life with Ronnie. So that takes care of Lotty, and brings us back to Grant. If you don't go up and see him today, he'll sign the house away tomorrow. As I see it, there's no reason why he shouldn't hand it over to Mrs. Peel for her lifetime, just as it stands. If she cleared out the junk, there'd be room to make it into a quiet little country hotel; she likes housework and she's a good manager, and she'd probably make a success of it as a business venture. But as a complete and final handover – no."

"Not even," Claire asked, "if it was a case of . . . of exorcising?"

He said nothing for a time.

"I forgot one thing," he told her at last, "and that was that you disliked the house. I forgot that you wouldn't mind seeing it go. And I forgot something else: your probable views on money and property. Your father's rich, isn't he?"

"Fairly."

"I'm glad its fairly; there are families who couldn't

LETTER TO MY LOVE

claim that they came by it that way. The only daughter of a rich father – how can I expect to make you see it my way? Your mind doesn't run on finance – but mine does. Grant has no right to hand over something his mother left him, simply to smooth out a temporary tangle in his mind. That kind of cure turns out in the end to be worse than the disease. One morning, he'll wake up and realize what he's done."

"Mrs. Peel could leave it back to him in her Will."

"That's what she's probably planning. She has no children, so back it can go when she's dead – she thinks. But if she hasn't children, she has relations – fairly close ones. They're not rich; in fact, they're poor. A valuable property like this one will bring them a-running to sun themselves in the glow of the gold. However decent they may be and probably are, it's a thousand to one, ten thousand to one that in the twenty years more she'll doubtless live, Grant will have faded out and left deserving brothers and sisters in his place. Now do you see?"

"Yes, I see. What do you expect me to do – go to Grant's flat this evening and tell him all this?"

"You've got to."

"Aren't you the one he's always listened to?"

"This time, he won't. I talked myself out last night. In the end, I dried up – not only because I'd argued myself to a standstill, but also because I realized that this thing is – has become – pathological. You can't reach him any more by appealing to his sense – all that's left is to put it on a

135

lower level and appeal to his senses, and that's where you come in."

"Thank you."

"You won't be so proud when your children ask you why you let their father throw away forty thousand pounds. My God! I hated Mrs. Tennant, but at this moment, I feel sorry for her. If Grant casts out a devil by giving away her house, he'll most surely raise a ghost – her ghost. She'll walk, that I'll swear. She'll – Why – " he broke off to ask, "are you looking at me with so puzzled an air?"

"Are you really so fond of Grant?"

He stared out at the quiet, narrow country road.

"It must be a father complex," he said. "I can't tell you what a hell of a shock it was to come back to England and find him in the state he's in. I knew, of course, that to a certain depth, there was softness – but I didn't know it went so deep. I'd always seen him give in to his mother up to a certain point – but after that, and especially in my case, he'd take up a position from which she couldn't shift him. But now . . ."

"He said he felt different in Canada – freer, stronger. Why can't you let him go back there in peace?"

"I will – if only he doesn't charge himself forty thousand pounds for the pleasure of going. You won't do anything?"

"No. In a way," she said slowly, "I agree with everything you've said – but to stop Grant from signing away the house is something I can't do. He may regret it one day, but we all have to do things we regret. Mrs. Tennant wouldn't have liked it, but Mrs. Peel served her well in that house, and perhaps it's a kind of justice that she should have it. I'm sorry I can't turn myself into a more forceful character, and go up there and make Grant see what you call reason. Certainly I couldn't do it in the way you suggested – if I didn't mistake what you said."

"I asked you to—"

"– make love to him, to bring him to a state in which he'd sign – or not sign – anything. Even if I wanted to, which I don't, I couldn't do it. I haven't got the . . . the equipment, for one thing."

"Haven't you?" He spoke absently, his eyes on her face. With a gentle forefinger, he traced its lines. "No equipment? You've got more than equipment. You've got weapons here you've never used. You've got charm and beauty, and a grace and a remoteness that so few, so very few women have now. For a whole Englishman, I think you're too remote; a whole Englishman would never reach you. But I'm only half an Englishman and I . . . I could reach you. I could find my way through the cool, shady approaches to the warm, the sunlit places. Claire" – he cupped her face in his hands and spoke softly – "I could. I could . . ."

She was in his arms. For timeless seconds, he held her and she lay unresisting against him. A warmth, a fire spread slowly through her body; through it she heard his voice murmuring her name.

And then she was abruptly released. She turned to look at him, and he spoke in a low, even voice.

"All right; you needn't say anything," he said. "You don't have to put it into words. I'm a . . . I'm anything you like to call me. You're going to marry my best friend and I take you out and make love to you. I mention him with affection, and then I tell you that I love you. I get you alone and lay unsanctified hands on you. I'm sorry. No, I'm not sorry. My only regret is losing sight, for a few moments, of Grant."

He started the engine. Beside him, Claire clenched her hands tightly together in her lap and struggled back to sanity. There was a mist before her eyes, and her heart was thudding violently; it was difficult to breathe. But to her infinite relief, she realized, moment by moment, that she could find her way back to her course by means of a well-defined chart. Grant. Wedding. Canada. House. Wedding. Grant. The channel was clearly marked. If she did not follow it, she would be lost indeed.

Grant. Wedding. Canada.

"Please," she heard him say, "don't be angry."

With a last great effort, she found her voice.

"Why not?"

She sounded, to her infinite relief, cool, composed.

"Well, be angry – but be forgiving, too. And remember that you were in my mind for a long time before I met you. I liked you. You were a girl who'd seen below Grant's surface deficiencies; you didn't wait for him to become eloquent or knight-in-armour. You loved him."

"Yes, I loved him."

But not any more, her heart cried. Not any more, not any more . . .

Grant. Wedding. Canada.

"After lunch – which we're going to have looking on to a calm blue sea – what would you like to do?" he asked.

"I'd like to go home."

"Then you shall go home. And Grant will have the papers drawn up ready for signing tomorrow."

"And perhaps when the house has gone, his devil will go and he'll be happy. Are you going to talk to him about it again?"

"No. Not any more."

They lunched at a quiet table and looked out at the sea, and nothing more was said of the house.

"What would you like to talk about?" Richard asked. "Food? Plays? Films?"

She made an effort.

"France. Do you like it better than England?"

"If you mean do I feel like a Frenchman – no. But, like my mother, I seem to need international society – many races, many tongues. Paris offers more of it than London."

"What exactly do you do?"

"Figures. Not human figures – the one-two-three sort. My mother hoped I'd be artistic, and so I am. I'm an artist with figures. Where other figure-men use their heads, I use a kind of instinct. I'm a figure-wonder. Which is a pity, in a way, because they send me here and there, far and wide, to expose poor devils who've been filching the firm's profits. I don't have to go through the books; I simply open them, look, and point. As I said, an artist. Sometimes I long to take the malefactors aside and explain just how they could have done it without detection – or without such rapid detection. As the cops are called, I find myself saying the old piece about there-but-for-the-grace-of-God; if my nature hadn't been so upright, what might I not have performed in the way of artistic embezzlement?"

"Where do you live? I mean, whereabouts in Paris?"

"If you left the Louvre and took the most direct line to the Seine, plunged in and swam across, I'd be waiting for you on my little flowerdecked balcony. I live in, and eat out. They still eat much better over there than they do over here. They also enjoy themselves more. There's a sort of inner spring of happiness that bubbles up in the French and not in the English. The English enjoy specific things like comfort, or money, or luxury, or travel – but in my humble and probably erroneous opinion, it's only the cockney who really enjoys himself as opposed to enjoying something outside himself."

She knew that he was talking to prevent himself from thinking. Some saving instinct made her able to adopt his own light tones. The brief episode by the roadside was fading . . . Not until they were near her home did he speak once more of Grant.

"Did you try," he asked, "to keep him in England?"

"There was no question of trying. He put it to me as a fact: he was going. All I had to do was decide whether I wanted to leave England and go with him. I don't want to leave England – but I do want to go with him."

She listened to the faint echo of the words, and was proud of the calm finality with which they were spoken. She seemed to herself to have become two people with two voices that disagreed violently – but only one of the voices was audible.

He did not come into the house. She stood on the drive and watched him get into the car.

"Thank you," she said, "for the lunch – and for other things."

"Such as—?"

"Trying to make things right for Grant. Are you going back to London?"

"I might." He paused before starting the engine. "There was something I wanted to ask your stepmother – but your aunts arrived this morning and" – he nodded towards the Daimler – "they're still here. It was something about the hospital."

"What about the hospital?"

"Well, the most damnable thing. They wouldn't let me in. I went to see old Corinne, and a slip of a nurse asked me what my name was, and then said nothing doing. Could you ask your stepmother to ring up and tell them that I'd like to see the poor old girl before I go back to France?"

"I'll tell her."

A letter. An old woman with a letter. A frightened old woman . . .

He was watching her with a frown.

"Look – what's behind this?" he asked. "If she's ill, I

141

ought to see her. If she's dying, she'd like to see me. But yesterday, in this house, when I mentioned going to see her, there was . . . *something*. You and your stepmother both. I thought it was my imagination until I got to the hospital. If there's any reason for keeping me out, I ought to know it. She's without close relations in this country and she was with Lotty and myself all my life. If you don't know why nobody can get in, I'll come into the house and wait while your stepmother rings up and asks them."

His hand was on the door. Claire spoke slowly.

"You won't be allowed in to see her," she said, "because they think she's . . . they have reason to believe she's frightened of you."

She saw a look of stupefaction come over his face – and then he gave a short, derisive laugh.

"*Frightened?* Rot! Old Corinne – frightened of me? If she is, her brain's given way and I'd like to see the doctors about it. Can't your stepmother arrange it?"

"There's a . . . a letter."

He stared at her uncomprehendingly.

"There's a what?"

"She's got a letter."

"Who has?"

"Corinne."

"Corinne . . . a *letter*? Are you trying to say—"

"She was brought to the hospital. She'd had a stroke. She's recovering, but all they know is that she's hidden a letter and your name seems to send her into a state of terror. So they won't let you in."

"They will let me in." He spoke calmly, but there was the beginning of uneasiness in his eyes. He stared at Claire, and she saw the uneasiness turn to something like fear. But he said nothing. Without a word of farewell, he started the car and drove swiftly away, and she turned and went up to her room.

To be alone – to think. But it was better, she found at once, not to think; it was better not to be alone. She would do better to go downstairs and talk to her aunts. She could help her stepmother – and help herself.

She regretted her decision when she saw her stepmother's clear-seeing gaze on her. She hadn't had a nurse's training for nothing, Claire realized. She could obviously see the cracks on the surface; one could only hope she couldn't see anything below the surface.

It seemed many hours before the Daimler was brought round and Netta and Ettie were settled in it. It bore them away, as it had brought them, with slow dignity, and Claire turned to her stepmother.

"Tired?" she asked.

"No. You must always remember that I had a long, hard training. Come inside" – she led Claire into the house – "and tell me what's the matter with you. Something's upset you. Was it Richard?"

"Yes and no. But just before he was going away, he told me that he'd tried to get into the hospital to see his old nurse – and hadn't succeeded."

"Did you tell him about the letter?"

"Yes. He looked astounded, and then he laughed."

But later, she remembered, he had looked uneasy . . . almost afraid . . .

"You look," she heard her stepmother say, "as though you ought to be in bed. Let me send your dinner up."

"No, thank you; I'm all right"

After dinner, she went to her father's room; he was already in bed, propped against snowy pillows, awaiting his warm milk. She stood by him – he disliked people sitting on his bed – and took his hand.

"Tired, darling?" she asked.

"A little." He sighed faintly; he looked like a saint meditating. "I don't like to see my sisters growing so frail."

"But they're well – and active. We did a lot while I stayed with them."

"They do too much."

"Would you like me to read to you?" She picked up the books that lay on his bedside table: Proust, Thomas Mann, and a surprisingly light new-comer. "Mystery and adventure?" she teased.

"Your stepmother" – he sounded vaguely displeased – "finds reading aloud tiring unless the books are . . . undemanding. No, thank you, I don't want to be read to."

She bent over and kissed the broad, noble brow, and felt a moment's wild impulse to tap it to find out whether it gave off a hollow sound.

"Sleep well, darling."

She went up to her room and walked over to the dressing-table and stared at Grant's photograph. She had always had a habit, she reminded herself, of panicking at the last moment. Before parties, before school departures, before examinations. Then she had found that the parties had been fun; she had enjoyed school once she got there – and she had passed the examinations. It was too much to expect that she could get through marriage without experiencing similar sensations. She loved Grant. For a little while, in the car, a man had touched her and her body had taken fire. But one could not alter one's entire life because passion had made an unheralded and fleeting appearance. She loved Grant.

She slept dreamlessly, and woke later than usual. After breakfasting alone, she went in search of her stepmother.

"Any plans?" she asked.

Mrs. Marston's eyes, taking in the signs of strain, led her mind to a swift and accurate diagnosis. But all she said was:

"We could go and have lunch out somewhere, if you felt like it. Your father won't be getting up today; yesterday tired him, although of course he won't admit that he finds his sisters exhausting."

They drove to a roadside inn; after lunch, they drove home and worked together in the garden. They had tea on the lawn in the sunshine and dinner on a table in front of the drawing-room fire, with rain beating on the windows. They talked of fashion, of flowers, of ocean and air travel, of music, of pictures. Not once was there a mention of Grant, or of marriage, or of Canada. There was no speculation, useless and worrying, over Wills. Nobody mentioned a letter. Claire's heart went out in gratitude to her step-mother who was, she knew, deliberately avoiding all but safe, tried topics, who by the end of the day had soothed her, charmed her out of her depression and given her courage to face whatever the future might bring. It was a day of respite.

Only when at last they parted in the hall, Mrs. Marston to go to her husband, Claire to go upstairs to bed, was the day's peace shattered, splintered.

The telephone rang, and Mrs. Marston walked over to answer it.

"You'd better wait a moment; it'll probably be for you," she said.

It was not for Claire. At her stepmother's low, in-credulous cry, she turned and waited, her hand gripping the balustrade. There were no words to be heard – only a feel-ing of dread, of sick anticipation. She heard her stepmother put down the receiver, and waited, her eyes upon her white, shocked face.

"Who?" Claire asked, speaking with difficulty.

"The hospital. He . . . he got in. They . . . He went between half past seven and eight – the only half-hour in the day when there isn't a nurse on duty at the door – only a doorman. The off-duty nurses were at supper; the two nurses on duty on her floor were busy with another patient. He gave his name and insisted on seeing his . . . his old nurse. He persuaded the doorman to go and fetch a nurse, and when the doorman went, he walked along the corridor until he found her name – and went in."

146

There was a long silence. Claire closed her eyes and saw him opening a door . . .

"And then?" she heard herself asking.

"The nurses heard her screaming. They rushed to the room, but all they heard was the sound of the car driving away."

"Did he . . . did he get the letter?"

"No."

Claire said nothing. She turned and walked slowly to her room and went in and closed the door.

CHAPTER EIGHT

THROUGHOUT her life, Claire had heard the sea murmuring or splashing or battering against the rocks that lay almost beneath her windows, but the sounds had never been more than an accompaniment to her thoughts or dreams. Tonight, lying sleepless, she gave her mind for the first time to the rising wind and the increasing restlessness of the waves, counting the moments between the swift uprush to the rocks and the boiling, hissing retreat. Crash, silence and splash; roar, uprush and angry return. It was better to listen than to think.

To think . . . of a man invading the sickroom of an old, defenceless woman. To think of a man who, under cover of furthering Grant's interests, made love to Grant's future wife.

Lying. Cheating. He had left her with the sound of passion still in her ears – and then he had tricked his way into the hospital in an attempt to wrest a letter from a frightened old woman.

The letter. He had known that it had some connection with Mrs. Tennant's last tragic hours. He had known, but he had lied.

Some time towards morning, she slept. She awoke to a day dark with rain clouds; gusty showers spattered against her windows. It was almost ten o'clock; there was a long day to be got through, another long night to be faced.

She went downstairs, drank some coffee, and then paid her morning visit to her father.

"Margaret has gone out to do a little shopping," he told her. "I didn't think she ought to go out in this heavy rain, but she wanted to look into the library and bring me something new to read."

But the books were on the table in the hall, and the maid had reported that the car had turned away from the town . . .

She stayed in the quiet, comfortable room for a time, adjusting a curtain, making up the fire, putting the newspapers closer at hand, her movements quiet and controlled, careful as usual to avoid any noise or brusqueness that could jar her father's sensibilities. Then she left him, and thereafter moved swiftly and purposefully. She was still buttoning her mackintosh as she climbed into the high, out-of-date car and backed it out of the garage. She drove fast. Ahead, in the hospital, a woman held a secret, and she was certain that her stepmother had gone to find out what it was.

That she was there, Claire was certain, even before she entered the wide drive of the hospital and saw the little black car parked outside the building.

And beside it, Richard's . . .

There was nothing to check her at the door; yes, Mrs. Marston was in Number Four; if she would go down the corridor and knock, she would be told whether she could go in or not.

Claire walked to the door, opened it, and went in.

Two people stood beside the bed: her stepmother, and Richard Tennant. Between them lay a long, emaciated figure, and Claire, who had never looked on death, did not need to be told that she was looking on it now.

She stared, horror-stricken, at the dead woman's face. Hollow cheeks, fallen in, shapeless lips, sparse, pitiful strands of hair. This was the woman whose screams had brought nurses running to aid her. This was the woman from whom a man, young and strong and ruthless, had attempted to drag a letter.

She saw Richard put out a hand and draw the sheet gently over the dead face. Then his eyes came up to meet the horror in her own.

"You . . . you killed her," she said.

He seemed unmoved.

"No. But I was here when she died."

"You wanted the letter."

"Yes."

"And you . . . you got it."

He hesitated, and then shook his head.

"I told you before," he said in the same level tones, "that it—"

"You said that it had nothing to do with the Will. That was a lie, wasn't it?"

"Could we say that it was a mistake?"

"That letter was the reason the Will was changed."

His face, which had been grey and drawn, lost the last vestige of colour.

"Yes."

"Then you must give it to me. I have a right to see it, and so has Grant." She held out a hand. "Will you please give it to me?"

He shook his head, this time decisively.

"No," he said. "I'm afraid I can't do that."

Mrs. Marston spoke for the first time.

"You must let her see it," she said. "Please give it to her."

He turned to look at her. Nothing was said, and Claire could not find out what he read in her stepmother's eyes. But slowly, he put his hand into his pocket, and drew out not one letter, but two. One was written on the thick white paper with the Spenders House heading. The other was a single sheet of very thin blue paper, with lines. The writing on it was large and bold, but in faded and almost indecipherable pencil. He held the blue sheet out to Claire, and she took it, and read it.

It was in French; brief, but long enough to reveal a man's heart.

"My own Lotty,

My own. How often did I say this when you were in my arms? My own. Mine. And how much more mine now that you hold my son under your heart? For yes, he will be a son, and we shall call him Paul, after me.

When I read your letter, when I knew that we were

*to have this son, I wept. And then I prayed. And then I
danced.*

*Lotty, Lotty, Lotty, I must see you. I cannot wait until
you come. I shall come to you. I shall come to England
and we shall be married. When you have read this letter,
look out of your window and I shall be there, to claim
you and to claim my son. I am glad that Corinne is with
you, and that she knows. I told Richard. He did not
weep or dance or pray but he said yes, he must be called
Paul Richard.*

My darling, God be with you always. I am coming.
Paul."

Richard's voice broke the silence.

"He didn't come," he said. "I saw him off at Orly Airport. The plane didn't crash; it was a less dramatic end.
When he landed in England, he couldn't wait for the usual
means of transport; he bought a motor-bike in London and
he was killed on his way to Spenders. I didn't know.
Corinne didn't know – but, somehow, Lotty knew. There
was no way of getting news; he was a Frenchman on a
visit, and nobody had any idea where he was going to
when he crashed. But Lotty knew that he was dead. She
came over to me and she stayed with me until the news of
his death reached his parents in Paris. She stayed with me –
and then Geoff Summerhill, who loved her, came over to
try and persuade her to marry him. She said she would – if
he would be a father to Paul's son. And he was – until he,
too, died."

"And Grant's mother" – Claire took up the tale in a toneless voice – "knew nothing until she found this letter. She loved Lotty's son because—"

"Because she thought he was Geoffrey's; yes. She found the letter, and in a blind rage, she decided that she and Grant were the only two people in the house who hadn't been in the secret – in the conspiracy. She was sure that Mrs. Peel had known – and Pierre. She knew she could get even with them, but the one she wanted to hurt most was Corinne. So she wrote to her and she sent her Lotty's letter. You needn't read the letter she wrote; it can be told in one word: hate. She told her that it was clear that everybody but herself knew the truth and that Lotty and Paul would get nothing more from her. She meant to change her Will, go back to the house and tell them what she'd done, and turn them out there and then."

"And when you heard that an old woman in this hospital had a letter—"

"No. Things were falling into place before that. Mrs. Peel's story about receiving a letter and writing a letter – at first it looked like nothing more than a grim coincidence – but I came to realize that it might be something more. If the letter Mrs. Tennant had received, or found, was Lotty's letter, who would be the first she'd hit out at? Corinne, who loved Lotty, who had guarded Lotty, fought for Lotty. If on that last morning Mrs. Tennant had written a letter, I thought that the person she must have addressed it to would be Corinne. I was right. Corinne got the letter and set out on a bitter morning for the telephone booth in the village – not to telephone, but to telegraph – to me. She didn't get to the phone. She was brought here, and . . . you know the rest. She clung to the letter because she knew that its loss would mean Lotty's betrayal."

"And you wanted it because you knew that it accounted for the change of Will. But you wouldn't have shown it to Grant."

"No, I wouldn't."

"You . . ." She paused; pain was tightening her throat. But when she went on speaking, it was in a cold, factual, relentless tone. "You didn't want Grant to see it because you didn't want him to know the truth. Not the truth about Lotty, but the truth about Paul. You tried to stop Grant from making the house over to Mrs. Peel; when you didn't succeed, you came and asked me to help you. You didn't want Mrs. Peel to have the house, but you wouldn't have raised any objections if Grant had then decided to give it over to Paul. But if Grant had seen this letter, he would have known that Paul had no claim to the house, because he wasn't Geoffrey Summerhill's son. And so you had to get the letter. And" – her glance went for a moment to the sheeted figure on the bed – "you got it. And in getting it, you killed a harmless old woman."

"I warned you once before," he said, "about letting your imagination run away with you." He put out a hand and took the letter from her. "Your summing-up is somewhat wide of the mark. It would be better if you didn't repeat it to Grant."

"Grant has a right to know the truth."

"Of course. Whether it would be right to tell him is another thing."

"You don't want him to know, because if he knows, he'll know the kind of man you are."

"If you care to put it that way – yes. If we're speaking of rights, I haven't any right to ask you – but I hope you won't tell him. If you'll agree to that, I'll go back to Paris today and you'll both be free of me. He's down at Spenders giving the house away – you said yourself it was his way of . . . of driving out the devil. Let him do it in his own way. Will you agree not to tell him?"

She looked at him; he was colourless, but entirely calm.

"I won't tell him," she said, "until we're . . . until he's had time to forget all he's been through since his mother died. I won't tell him that you . . ."

She stopped. Her stepmother's hand closed firmly over her arm.

"Claire – come with me."

Claire turned to her.

"He lied and lied – to me. He cheated. He—"

She was stopped by the sound of a quietly-closing door.

He had gone. He had gone, and with him the letter which had betrayed Lotty. She was left with her stepmother and with the dead woman who had tried to guard Lotty's secret.

"Claire—" Mrs. Marston began.

Claire broke in abruptly.

"I'm going down to Spenders," she said. "Grant's down there – he's seeing Mrs. Peel and the lawyers. I'm going to tell him that I'll marry him and go to Canada with him."

"Later, Claire," her stepmother begged. "You're not giving yourself time to think."

"Think about what? We know everything now. We know why that Will was made."

"Are you going to—"

"— tell Grant? No. He's found his own way of getting back his peace of mind and I'm not going to do anything to shatter it. I'd like to be there when he signs the house away. When it's gone, he'll be free and we can both get away from it all — and forget. The one thing I can leave Grant is his feeling for Richard. Let him go on thinking he's . . . upright and honourable."

Her stepmother looked at her for a few moments without speaking.

"I didn't know you could be so hard," she said at last.

"What do you want me to do? Forget what Richard did? Forget all his lies and—"

"I wasn't thinking about forgetting. I was thinking about forgiving."

Claire's eyes went to the figure lying under the sheet. Then she looked at her stepmother.

"Was the visit last night," she asked, "was the fact that she was shocked and frightened, was the attempt to force her to give up the letter the cause of her death?"

Mrs. Marston frowned.

"She was extremely ill. She—"

"You said that she was recovering. Did the visit cause her death?"

"How can one say for certain what—"

"In your own, your professional opinion, did it cause her death?"

"I'd—"

"Yes or no?"

"Yes," said Mrs. Marston.

"That's all I wanted to know."

"But Claire, if you like someone, love someone—"

"What," asked Claire coldly, "has that to do with the present circumstances?"

There was a long, tense silence, and it became clear at last that Mrs. Marston was not going to end it. Without saying any more, Claire turned and walked out to the car and drove down to Spenders, and it seemed like a continuation of her thoughts to see Lotty coming out at the sound of her arrival.

"Claire . . . I thought it was Grant."

"Isn't he here?"

"He came down this morning, and then he went into Spenders to see the lawyers about the house – about making it over to Mrs. Peel."

Claire went into the hall, and looked round it for what she hoped would be almost the last time.

"Did Mrs. Peel go with him?" she asked.

"No. She doesn't have to go until it's all ready to sign. But . . . well, she isn't terribly well."

"Where is she – in bed?"

"No. She was all right until . . . Well, to be quite honest, I upset her. I gave her a shock."

Claire walked slowly into the drawing-room.

"What kind of shock?" she asked.

Lotty hesitated. She was wearing a pale-green cotton dress and white sandals and looked nineteen and virginal. And she had loved, and it was Paul, and not Geoffrey Summerhill, who had been in Richard's mind when he had spoken of her love and of her loss. Paul, father of another Paul . . .

"I suppose you know that I'm going to marry Ronnie?" Claire heard her asking.

"Yes."

"Well, before I said I'd marry him, I told him . . . But perhaps you'll get a terrible shock and feel ill, like Mrs. Peel. I don't see that it matters any more if a few people — people like her and you and Grant — know the truth now. I told her that Paul wasn't Geoffrey Summerhill's son. He was the son of a man I loved in Paris. A man who died before we could marry. Geoff knew, and now Ronnie knows. But Mrs. Peel . . . I suppose she felt I shouldn't have deceived Mrs. Tennant for all those years. I wouldn't have done if Geoff hadn't insisted on saying nothing. Perhaps he knew he wasn't going to live long. Some people do know about dying. I think I'll know, when the time comes. I knew about Paul's father. I think Geoff must have known about himself, and he wanted to make sure that Mrs. Tennant would look after us. He wasn't frightened of her, like Grant; he wouldn't have been afraid to tell her — but it was too great a risk, he said. 'She loves Paul, and it would be cruel to tell her the truth.' So I didn't."

"Where is Mrs. Peel?"

"In the kitchen."

Mrs. Peel was experiencing what must have been a deep emotional crisis – but when Claire found her, she was standing at the sink peeling potatoes. Work had to go on; food had to be prepared; Mrs. Tennant was dead and there was time enough to worry about what this piece of news would have done to her . . .

But Claire was unprepared for the ravaged face that was turned to hers when she entered.

"Oh – Claire." Mrs. Peel reached absently for a towel and, having dried her hands, held it as if uncertain what to do with it. Claire took it from her and hung it up, and then dragged a chair nearer.

"Sit down," she said. "You look ill."

Mrs. Peel waved the chair aside and raised a haggard face.

"You saw Lotty?"

"Yes."

"She didn't by any chance tell you – what she told me?" Claire hesitated.

"Look, couldn't I bring you a drink? You—"

"You've got something to tell me."

"Yes. But—"

"I can stand it. After Lotty's little piece of information, I can stand anything. Seven years – nearly eight. Dear Lord, if Grant's mother had known—"

"She did know."

159

Silence fell. After what seemed an age, Mrs. Peel took a deep breath, and squared her shoulders.

"Go on," she said hardily. "Tell me. You say she knew. How did she know and how do you know that she knew?"

"Lotty lost a letter. It was a letter written by Paul's father just after Lotty had written to tell him she was to have his child. He came over to England, but he was killed in a road accident before he got to Spenders. Lotty kept the letter, but just before Mrs. Tennant died, she must have found it. She sent it to Lotty's old nurse, with a covering letter saying that it was clear that everybody in the house had known the truth – except herself and Grant. She was going to turn you all out, but she died before she could come back to the house and do it. She—"

"How do you know this?"

"I've just come from the hospital. Lotty's old nurse – Corinne – is dead. She died this morning."

"And the letter . . ."

"Richard has the letter."

Mrs. Peel stared at her.

"*Richard?* How does—"

"My stepmother told me that there was an old woman in the hospital who seemed to have some connection with him – who seemed to be afraid of him. The hospital staff had orders not to let him in if he went to see her. He didn't know, at first, that she was there – but he did know that Lotty had lost a letter that would have told Mrs. Tennant the truth about Paul; he knew that you had seen Mrs. Tennant with a letter. When he found that the woman in

160

the hospital was his and Lotty's old nurse, when he learned that she had a letter she was anxious to hide, he . . . he guessed it must be Lotty's letter. He went to see her once, but they wouldn't let him in."

"Richard . . . went to the hospital?"

"Yes. Once unsuccessfully – and again last night."

"Last night? He . . ."

"He went to the hospital between half past seven and eight, when there was only a doorman on duty. He sent him away to fetch a nurse, and then he . . ." She closed her eyes for a moment to shut out agonizing memories – "and then he went into her room and they heard her screaming . . . but they didn't see Richard."

"Then how—"

"He gave the doorman his name. I went to the hospital this morning. He was there with my stepmother. He had the letter – Lotty's letter . . . just a thin blue sheet of paper. I read it, and—"

She stopped. Mrs. Peel had put out a hand and caught her arm in a tight, painful grip.

"Claire, I . . ."

Her voice was hoarse; her face was so deathly white that Claire led her to the chair, placed her on it and went swiftly to the drawing-room, returning with a glass in her hand.

"Drink this." She held it to Mrs. Peel's lips until the last drop was finished. "Would you like me to take you upstairs? You look very ill."

"I – yes, I'm ill. I've got to be by myself for a little while. I've got to . . . I can't stand any more. I'm not young,

F   161

and I can't . . . I've had enough shocks." She put her hands to her head and gave a low moan. "I've . . . I've got to think. I must think. I . . . oh, Claire, don't tell Grant! Promise me you won't tell him?"

"I promised Richard I wouldn't tell him," Claire said, and found Mrs. Peel staring at her with an almost wild gaze.

"He asked you . . . Richard asked you not to—"

"He didn't want Grant to know, and I promised not to tell him. At any rate, not yet."

There was a long silence. Mrs. Peel got heavily to her feet, and the younger woman looked at her anxiously.

"Let me go up with you and—"

"No. Will you" – her hand made a vague gesture indicating the preparations for lunch – "will you take over for a while?"

"Yes. Can I bring you up something?"

"I don't want food or drink. I want to be by myself. I want to be left absolutely alone."

"You were going this afternoon—"

"To the lawyers. They can wait. If I don't lie down, I shall break down. I only ask you, for God's sake, not to tell Grant what you've just told me . . ."

"I've told you I won't."

"Thank you." She turned from the door and looked back at Claire with a curiously pitying look. "You've had a bad time through it all," she said. "Right from the start, you've been in it."

"Yes. But it's over."

162

Mrs. Peel made no reply; she closed the door behind her and Claire heard her going upstairs. She took off her coat, put on an apron, and was busy at the stove when Grant came in.

"Mrs. Peel isn't feeling well," she said, before he could speak. "You needn't be worried about lunch – I can cook."

Her voice – she listened to it in amazement – was calm and untroubled. He did not answer, and she went up to him and put her arms round him and laid her head on his shoulder.

"You look tired," she said.

"I saw Lotty. She said she'd told you – and told Mrs. Peel."

"Yes."

"No wonder" – his voice was bitter – "no wonder she feels ill. Claire—"

"You needn't say it," she said gently. "You've had enough, and so have I. We've both had enough. If you want to marry me, I'll marry you on one condition, and that is that you take me to Canada as soon as we can get married and go."

She could not see his face. She could only feel the deep, long breath that spoke of his relief, of the easing of tension, of a dawning hope for the future.

"I love you," he said unsteadily. "But—"

"Not today," she begged. "Say it again – and leave it at that."

"I love you," he said.

CHAPTER NINE

CORINNE REMINGTON'S funeral took place two days later, in the cemetery at Gisborough. Claire's stepmother, leaving the house on what seemed to be a normal morning's shopping, said nothing until her return of the real reason for her absence; then she told Claire quietly in the drawing-room.

Talking to Claire since the morning of Corinne's death had not been an easy matter; Mrs. Marston could not even be sure if she heard what was being said. There had been, between them, no exchanges beyond those relating to household matters; after dinner, Claire had gone straight to bed. She spoke to her now without any hope of arousing any sign of interest.

"Lotty's old nurse was buried today."

"I imagined," Claire said, "that that's where you'd gone."

"My black suit?"

"And the feeling that you'd go to the funeral."

"There were only two cars. Richard and Lotty and Pierre were in the first. I followed with Ronnie Pierce."

There was a flicker of surprise, but Claire said nothing.

"No questions?" her stepmother asked.

"No. I told you — it's over. What's the use of remembering any of it? I can't quite see why Ronnie Pierce should have been there."

"He was married to Lotty yesterday, in London."

"I see. I hope they'll be happy."

Her stepmother's eyes rested on the pale, tired face and she spoke abruptly.

"I'm not concerned about their happiness," she said. "I'm only concerned about yours. I can't bear to see you like this."

Something in her voice — an affection deeper than Claire had realized — brought the colour into her cheeks.

"I told you," she said. "Everything's going to be all right."

"Everything isn't, Claire. Nothing can be right when you're marrying a man you don't love."

And there it was, Mrs. Marston thought with relief and satisfaction. It was said. Out loud. She had been longing to say it, but had lacked the courage to give it voice. Now she had brought it out; she had said it openly and baldly, though not in the way she had planned to say it as she had lain awake for the past two nights, worrying about her stepdaughter, worrying about her own authority, or lack of it.

She had married Claire's father and had promised to love and look after him; there was nothing in the contract that gave her the right to forbid his daughter to do whatever she wanted to do. Especially to forbid her to marry a man she had decided to marry.

She did not love him. But where – Mrs. Marston looked hopefully, longingly round the drawing-room – where was the man she did love? Where was the man who had declared quietly, dispassionately to her two mornings ago that he loved and longed for Claire?

He was in Paris. Or if not actually there, would be there before long. If he wouldn't speak, how could others speak for him?

They couldn't speak for him – but they could speak the truth, as she had spoken it to Claire a few moments ago. She had thrown out a challenge: a man you don't love. A man from whom you will never get the support you need. A man who failed you and who will fail you again – and again. A man who—

"You shouldn't," she heard Claire saying, "make too much of a moment's stupidity. Richard Tennant would be able to explain exactly how he managed to . . . upset me. He could explain the system; he's an expert."

"He loves you."

"So he told me. It wasn't, in the circumstances, much of a compliment."

"You love him."

Claire gave a brief, scornful smile.

"I'll get over it."

"Couldn't you wait? Couldn't you let Grant go to Canada and – and follow him later, if you wanted to?"

"Haven't I waited long enough? I'm grateful to you,

but it's no good. When Grant hands Spenders over to Mrs. Peel, we—"

"She isn't there."

Claire stared at her.

"Isn't where?"

"Mrs. Peel isn't at Spenders. She hasn't been there for the past three days."

Three days. . . .

"Where is she?"

"She came up to London."

"Who told you this?"

"Richard, this morning after the funeral."

Claire sat very still, her thoughts racing. Grant had gone down to Spenders to complete the formalities of handing over the house to Mrs. Peel. She had imagined that they were still there. But Mrs. Peel was in London, and Grant—

"You and Richard," she said slowly, "seem to know more—"

"– of what's going on than you do? Perhaps I ought to have told you before that he sent for me the other morning. From the hospital."

"You mean," Claire said after consideration, "that he found he couldn't get in to see her – and so he asked you to help him."

"Yes."

"And you . . . you let him into her room?"

"Yes."

There was a long silence.

"I don't understand," Claire said at last. "You told me

167

that he was at all costs to be kept away. He had got in once – by a trick. And you . . .''

''He sent for me. She was dying. I told him, when I got to the hospital, that I would keep him out at all costs. He didn't say anything except to ask me if I would go in to her and ask her if she wanted to see him.''

''*Wanted to see him?* And you went!''

''Yes. I went in and I took her hand and I asked her in the way he'd asked me to ask her. I asked her if she remembered the grotto and the bats and the chair on the terrace and the lilies of the valley. It didn't make any sense to me, but I said it as he had asked me to say it. She began to tremble, and she caught my hands, and said: 'Go and ask him what initials were on the tree, and what tree it was.' I asked him and he said it was a willow and the initials on it were L.A. When I told her, she raised herself on her pillows and began to call out in a terrible croaking voice.''

''Call out?''

''She called out his name, and he went in.''

She had called out his name and he had gone in. He had not broken in, forced his way in. He had sent her a message that she understood, and then another – and then she had called him and he had gone in.

And Mrs. Peel was not at Spenders' taking over the house. She was in London. And Lotty was married and was at Ronnie Pierce's farm, and Richard . . .

Richard had gone.

She came back to herself to find the door opening. A maid had come to say that a lady wished to see them. ''To

LETTER TO MY LOVE

see which of them?" Mrs. Marston inquired. "To see either," was the reply. "And the lady's name?"

"Mrs. Peel."

For a moment, as she entered the room, shock kept Claire rigid. The thin legs had always looked as though they belonged to someone else -- but now it seemed to her that, like the paper figures in some childish game, a face had been put on to the wrong body – a face sunken and white and pinched.

The visitor spoke quietly to Mrs. Marston.

"Don't go, please."

Claire scarcely recognized the voice, but there was authority in it. Mrs. Marston drew forward a chair; the three women sat down and looked at one another.

"You're ill," Mrs. Marston said. "You must let me send for—"

"No. I'm ill, but I don't want anything, thank you. I came here to say something that has to be said. When I've said it, I shall go away."

Mrs. Marston was not listening; she was pouring out a drink.

"When you've drunk that," she said, handing it to Mrs. Peel, "we'll listen to whatever you want to say. But not before."

They waited in silence until Mrs. Peel had drunk and handed back the glass.

"Now," Mrs. Marston said.

"I've been in London for three days – thinking." Her eyes rested on Claire. "You came down to Spenders three

169

days ago, and I went up to my room – but when I got there, I knew I had to get out of the house. I packed some things for the night – and I went up to London. When I got there, I didn't know where to go. Yes" – she corrected herself – "I knew where I had to go, but I sat on a bench at the station all the afternoon, all the evening, thinking there might be some other way. Then a . . . a woman policeman came up and spoke to me. I told her I was ill. She asked me if I had anywhere to go, and I said yes, and I got up and she put me into a taxi and I drove to Richard's hotel."

Silence fell, and lengthened, and at last the tired, lost voice took up the story.

"He wasn't there. He came back later and told me that he had been with Ronnie Pierce, arranging about a licence for Lotty's wedding. Then he said he would put me on the train and send me home. I said he didn't know why I'd come and he said yes, he did know. He said it was no use. He said talking wouldn't make things better, but worse. He said it was better to leave things as they were, straight and cleared up and no more tangles. For a little while, I believed him. For a little while, I told myself that perhaps he was right. And then . . . I knew he wasn't. You can't build a life on lies. You can't. You think you can, but you can't. But I didn't tell him that. I asked if he would let me stay there for a day or two, and he said he'd arrange it. He said he'd come back – but he didn't come back. He sent a letter and I got it this morning; he said that when I read it, Lotty would be married and safe, and he himself would be in Paris, and you . . . and you and Grant would marry and go away and everything would be forgotten. I read the letter – and then I came here. Because" – she stared at Claire as though seeing her for the first time – "I realized that it all depended on you. All I had to do was tell you, and because you loved him, you would understand. It would be up to you. That's what it all came down to, in the end: you."

She paused and then went on in a heavy, monotonous voice.

"When you came down to Spenders," she said, "and told me that Corinne was dead, I was feeling ill, because Lotty had just given me her shattering piece of news, and it had lodged itself in my head and was battering and battering until I thought I was going mad. Paul was not Geoffrey Summerhill's son. That was a staggering thing to have to believe, but beyond it there was something else – the letter. Lotty had lost a letter . . . a letter from Paul's father. When you told me that, I felt a sort of . . . I felt absolutely convinced that Mrs. Tennant had found it. She had found it and she had read it. It explained everything that had happened on the day she died.

"And then – I was left remembering the day before she died. I remembered that I had told Grant, who was at Spenders that week-end, that I couldn't find the papers his mother wanted – papers that had something to do with Geoffrey Summerhill. I remembered Grant's telling me that I'd been looking in the wrong places – the papers wouldn't be among his mother's, or his, papers, but among Lotty's.

He was right. The papers were there. I put them into a long envelope and I put the envelope on Mrs. Tennant's breakfast tray along with her other letters. Had I by some terrible chance put Lotty's letter into the envelope by mistake? Had the letter been among the papers or had I missed it? I didn't think so; there were only two or three documents and a paper or two; I'd opened everything to make sure that the documents were the correct ones. I didn't see a letter, but . . . could that be the explanation? Had I, without knowing it, given away Lotty's secret?

"It was a terrible thought. But not so terrible as what was to come. Because" – she was staring across the room and she had ceased to address Claire – "because later, when Claire came down, she told me that Corinne was dead, and she told me that Corinne had had the letter and that Richard had guessed, and Richard had got it. And then, without any warning, she told me what the letter was like. A thin blue sheet. A single thin blue sheet. And then I knew I'd seen the letter. And I knew where."

The room was very still.

"And in the end, I knew that I had to tell Claire. Loving you, she'll understand as I understand. She'll forgive, as I do. But she has to know that it wasn't I who looked for those papers in Lotty's desk. It was you. And when you brought them to me, I looked through them, and checked them, and then you said – Oh God, why did I have to remember? – you said you would put them into an envelope. And so I gave you the papers, and if you'd put them into an envelope straight away, I would never have

172

known. But you didn't. You must have fought it off for a little while. It wasn't until you were leaving the house that night that you made up your mind – and I don't know whether it was God's hand, or the devil's, that took me into your mother's study at the moment that you put the papers into a long envelope, that let me see you put in with the papers a thin, single blue sheet folded in half. You sealed the envelope, and I thought it natural at the time. Perhaps it seemed even more natural afterwards, when I understood. You thought your mother ought to know, and you took the only way you knew of telling her. You thought it was wrong to have deceived her – and so you let her read the letter. You couldn't know, you didn't know what it would do to her – or what she would do to us. You'd forgotten the Puritan streak in her. You acted without thought for anybody but your mother, who had been deceived, and Claire will forgive you. Dear Grant, Claire had to know.''

She paused, and her eyes went round the room as though she could not remember where she was. Then they came to rest on Claire, and she spoke to her quietly.

''You said that Richard had gone to the hospital three nights ago, between half past seven and eight. He didn't. He couldn't have been at the hospital because he was at Spenders with Lotty and with Ronnie Pierce and myself. He—''

''It was Grant,'' said Mrs. Marston, ''who went to the hospital. When Richard sent for me the next morning, and told me that he wanted to see Miss Remington, he said that he had not been there the night before. I believed him, but it was easy enough to prove. I sent for the doorman, and he gave a description of the man he had seen. But I think," she ended gently, "you guessed that it must have been Grant."

"He had to have the letter." Mrs. Peel addressed her in a voice of desperate appeal. "Don't you see? All he wanted to do when he first read Lotty's letter was to end what he must have seen as a wicked conspiracy against his mother. When he realized what effect it had had on her, his one idea was to . . . to make amends. He offered – Claire knows that he offered – to Lotty and Pierre and myself – everything his mother had promised. He gave up the house because he couldn't bear the terms under which he had inherited it. He was going away, leaving the house, leaving England. All he wanted to do was forget. But there was the letter."

"Yes," Mrs. Marston said. "There was the letter."

"We had given up . . . I had given up any hope of ever finding out the truth about the letter I saw Mrs. Tennant reading . . . until Claire mentioned an old lady in hospital and seemed to think that she had some connection with us. I found myself wondering afterwards whether . . . it didn't seem likely to lead to anything, but if it was Corinne . . . When Grant got in touch with me, I reminded him of what Claire had said, and asked him if he thought . . . But he said there was no use reopening the business of the letter – and so I put it out of my mind. But you can see that Grant might go on wondering – and might try to get

Lotty's letter back. You mustn't blame him too much for going to see Corinne" — she turned beseechingly to Claire — "you mustn't blame him for giving Richard's name. You understand, don't you?"

"Yes, I understand," Claire said.

"He never," Mrs. Peel said, "did a mean or a bad thing in his life. But he couldn't bear to see his mother . . . couldn't you call it 'victimized'?"

"You could," Claire said.

"I wanted to tell you everything, and that's why I came here. If you love people, Claire, you can forgive them."

"Yes," Claire agreed. "You can."

She got suddenly to her feet, and went blindly towards the door and out of the room.

She went towards the staircase, and then turned away. There was only one room in the house into which problems never entered. There was only one person in the house protected, sheltered from conflict and mental stress and unhappiness.

She knocked on her father's door and entered the silent, sunny room. Here, nothing would touch her. For a little while, she would be isolated, insulated from the trouble and confusion that lay outside.

"Have you," her father asked, "come to read to me?"

"If you like, darling. What shall I read?"

"There isn't much choice. One of those library books is in the form of letters, and the other is about horses."

Claire chose the horses, and sat down to read.

175

CHAPTER TEN

"R ICHARD knew," Claire said.

"Yes, he knew," said Mrs. Marston.

It was quiet in the green and white bedroom. Claire, sitting on the window seat, looked out and watched the sun sending a last glow over the shadowed sea. The sky was pale pink; across it lay smudges of cloud. The sea, still restless after the morning's wind, turned green and then grey. The sky darkened and the sails of little ships scudding homewards looked like paths faintly marked on a hilly road.

Mrs. Marston, sitting on the bed, looked almost beautiful in the soft light. Claire turned to speak to her.

"You knew," she said, "that morning in the hospital. You knew, and you let me believe that Richard—"

"All I knew then, Claire, was that Richard hadn't forced his way into her room. He knew nothing about it until he called at the hospital next morning – and ran into trouble. The doorman wasn't on duty, but his name was enough. He was told that his intrusion of the evening before had had a very serious effect on the patient. He guessed she was dying. He left the hospital and went to the nearest telephone and asked me to meet him. I was, he said, to say nothing to anyone. When I got to the hospital, he was waiting. He said that he had not been there the evening before; the only proof necessary was to send for the doorman, who said at once that he had never seen Richard before. He described the man he had seen, and Richard and I both knew it was Grant. But I was still afraid to let him into the room; if she saw anybody in her weak state who upset her, I would be answerable for the consequences. So he asked me to take her a message — and I did. She wouldn't, couldn't believe it was Richard; she had to send another message, to make sure. When he went in, she . . . she didn't have long, but he made that last hour happy for her. She died in his arms."

"And you knew all that, and you let me . . ."

"I promised Richard I would say nothing. He loved Grant, and he loved you and he wanted you both to be happy. He told me what Mrs. Peel told us both in the drawing-room today — that Grant had never done a mean or a wrong action in his life, and that he acted as he did only because he was horrified at finding out that young Paul was not Geoffrey Summerhill's son, nothing to do with Geoffrey, and had no claim to the affection his mother had lavished on him."

"You knew I didn't love Grant."

"I was almost sure you didn't. I was almost sure you loved Richard — but how could I be quite sure? I knew that he loved you — but how could I be sure that you hadn't been . . . swept off your feet? When I met him, saw his strength and charm and force and compared them with Grant's hesitations and weakness, I tried to warn you; I told you to keep away from him. I felt it was impossible for you to go on seeing him for long without growing to love him as he loved you. And when I saw you look at Richard over poor Corinne's body, look at him with horror, how could I be sure that any feeling you had for him would survive? I'm used to responsibility, heavy responsibility, but I'm not prepared to take the responsibility of telling a man that a woman loves him without seeing more proof of it than you showed that morning. Besides which, I felt that you were old enough to work the thing out for yourself; you're a woman of twenty-six and not a girl of sixteen. And lastly, I'm not your mother; I'm merely your stepmother."

Claire stared out once more over the darkening sea.

"Do you believe," she asked slowly, without turning, "that Grant acted on his mother's behalf?"

The pause that followed was so long that she turned.

"Well?"

"You knew him and I didn't," said Mrs. Marston. "You can make up your own mind. Richard believed in him. He said that Grant shouldn't be made to pay too highly for what he did."

"It depends, doesn't it, on what his motives were?"

"You're not suggesting that he was jealous of young Paul?"

"I'm not suggesting he was jealous of anybody — but I'm not prepared to accept the theory that he acted on

178

impulse. Mrs. Peel said that he found the letter in the morning, with the papers in Lotty's desk. He kept it all that day and didn't put it into the envelope until he left the house that evening. Is that impulsive?"

"No, but—"

"And I think that when he decided to let his mother see that letter, he wasn't thinking of young Paul. He wasn't thinking of anybody. He was only thinking about the house."

"I don't understand."

"Then let me explain. That morning – the day before Mrs. Tennant changed her Will and died – Richard had been at Spenders. He wasn't there long; he had a quarrel with Mrs. Tennant and left the house. The quarrel was over Lotty. Mrs. Tennant told him two things: that she had got rid of Ronnie Pierce, who had wanted to marry Lotty, and that she intended leaving Lotty – probably in trust for Paul – a share in the house. If she told Richard that, she certainly told Grant. And Grant realized for the first time that the house he loved so much would – might – never be wholly his. When his mother died, he and I wouldn't be able to live there and bring up our children there – or if we did, we wouldn't be able to have the whole of the house."

"He could have bought Lotty's share."

"You never saw Lotty's part of the house, and you don't know Lotty. As Grant saw it, there she was, settled for ever. As Grant saw it, his mother would and could get rid of any man who ever came after Lotty – because if she lost

Lotty, she lost Lotty's little boy. I can see — can't you? — that at her age, he meant a lot. Grant would marry and perhaps be lost to her in the way they say sons are lost when they marry — but Paul would grow up in her house and she would probably be dead long before the time came for him to marry and go away. The share in the house was a bribe for Lotty, and Grant must have visualized her settling down at Spenders for ever, taking more and more rooms for her pictures, growing more and more difficult to get rid of, or to buy out."

"And then, you're going to say, he found that letter, and saw a way out?"

"Yes. He hadn't the imagination to see what effect the letter would have on his mother — but he hadn't forgotten her Puritan streak. He not only remembered it — he was banking on it. His mother would — he thought — read the letter, and that would be the end of Lotty."

"And young Paul?"

"What did that matter? He could, he undoubtedly would make ample provision for Paul's future. All that mattered, all that would happen was that Lotty would have to go. And if she went, she would in all probability go to Ronnie Pierce, marry him, and give her son a good home and a good background. And room for all his animals. But Mrs. Tennant read the letter, and you know the rest. And when Grant went to the hospital, he didn't go because he wanted to get the letter in order to guard or to preserve Lotty's secret; he simply wanted to make sure that nobody would ever know what he had done."

"But you said yourself that he couldn't know how his mother would react to—"

"Are you on Richard's side, or on Grant's?"

"Perhaps on Grant's. Richard has so much. He has strength and confidence and a clear mind, and happy childhood memories, and lightness of heart. He loves you, but he had, and always will have a life of his own apart from you. But Grant . . ."

Tears began to course down Claire's cheeks, but she ignored them.

"Grant had health," she said, "and money, and a good job – and a woman who loved him."

"A mother he was afraid of, and a house he thought he would never own, never be his and yours and your children's. So in a moment of weakness, he—"

"It wasn't weakness. It was the only strong thing he ever did. He could be strong – under cover. If he had succeeded this time, he—"

"He wasn't," her stepmother reminded her gently, "a very proficient villain, Claire. Everything he did was—"

"There's always a first time. If it had succeeded, if it had come off, if it had paid off, Lotty would have been turned out and so would her son, and nobody would have known how Mrs. Tennant had found out, and he would have realized that cunning was a good enough substitute for courage."

"But even before he was found out—"

"His plan went wrong, and he lost his nerve. He thought

his mother would use a pruning knife, and she used a scythe. She mowed them all down. He got the house, but in reaching something down off the shelf, he'd pulled down a lot of other things and they'd fallen on him and hurt him."

"You're less generous than Richard."

"You told me once before," Claire said unsteadily, "that I was hard. You talked about forgetting. What you forget is that when I . . . when I said what I did, I was standing beside the bed of an old woman whose death I believed to have been hastened, or caused, by Richard. I had to face the fact that I had fallen in love with a man who was a liar and a cheat. So I faced it. And after facing it, I knew that I still loved him – but that I had to put him out of my mind. I didn't love Grant, but I thought I could help him, be happy with him. Is it being hard to decide, after this, that I can't marry him and can't be happy with him? I'm not judging. I'm not condemning. I'm only too glad, too happy, to know that Richard is . . . is . . ." She paused to steady her voice. "Richard knew Grant. I didn't. I fell in love with Grant because he was the first man I ever met who presented passion in an acceptable form. I wanted a man, I wanted marriage, I wanted children. But I wanted them on a basis I could handle. I thought I could do without passion – until I met Richard. I was never really in love – until I met Richard. You . . . you shouldn't have let him go away."

"I've told you why I let him go."

182

"Will he come back?"

"No," Mrs. Marston replied. "He won't come back."

There was a pause.

"In that case" – Claire spoke calmly and with finality – "I shall go to him."

CHAPTER ELEVEN

THERE was a sense of adventure in arriving at an airport, for the first time, without a ticket. There was something of change and interest in applying for a seat on the Paris plane, in being asked to wait, in learning after a prolonged interval that there was a vacant place. There was wonder in watching the weighing of her luggage, not, as on previous air journeys, a matter for anxiety on the score of overweight. It was difficult to believe that the small suitcase was her sole piece of luggage. It was fantastic to realize that she was at London Airport, aged twenty-six, and for the first time in her life travelling on her own initiative, with nobody to see her off – and nobody to meet her on arrival.

She had no plan, other than to reach Paris. He was there, and Lotty had given her two addresses; if he wasn't at his office, he would be at his flat. There was very little to be said. She loved him, she did not love Grant, she was not going to marry Grant. The rest could be said, or not said, by Richard. If the moment in the car had been for him, as for her, a shifting of the entire structure of life, there would perhaps be nothing more to say.

She sat quietly on a bench, watching the luggage being wheeled out to the aircraft. There went part one; part two, herself, would shortly follow the neat hostess and take the last-minute seat and count the time that must elapse before she saw Paris and Richard.

She heard, dimly and with a sense of dawning happiness, the flight number. So, perhaps, St. Peter would summon those outside the gates, and open them, and check the numbers of the new arrivals.

But in the meantime, she was to join the other passengers in Bay Number Four.

The neat – and very pretty – stewardess ran an eye over her charges.

"This way, please. Will you follow me?"

Claire took two steps in the wake of the group – and then took no more. A hand had closed round her arm. She was being turned slowly. She was face to face with Richard.

There was, she saw, no need to speak – but he was saying something.

"There are" – he led her in the direction of the exit – "telephones. And telegrams. And—"

"My – my luggage. They . . . it's on the plane."

"I hope it has a safe journey – there and back. As I was saying, people nowadays telephone, or send telegrams, or even write."

"How did you—?"

"Your stepmother, so much wiser, so much calmer, so much more economical than you, telephoned my office this

185

morning. I was in the middle of something particularly pressing, but I left it."

"When did you—"

"The plane from Paris – the one you're not on now – touched down an hour ago."

"But I've been here—"

"An hour ago. But I told myself that girls sometimes change their minds. They go so far – and then they don't go any farther. I could tell myself – watching you – that you looked very much in love, but I couldn't really be sure until you gave every sign of pushing past the other passengers in your anxiety to be first aboard. Then I knew that you were indeed going – and so I saved you the trouble – and the fare."

"My ticket—"

"The money will be refunded in due course. If you'll come this way, we'll collect my sparse luggage; I didn't have time to put in more than my wedding suit."

He led her outside in search of a car.

"There are coaches up to London," she pointed out. "You mentioned economy."

"Coaches don't go to Hallowes."

He chose a fast car with a stolid-looking driver. He put Claire into it and sat beside her and took her hand and held it lightly.

"There are," he told her, "before we begin to be happy, certain things to be said."

"Not now," she begged.

186

"I think yes, now. I wanted to say, chiefly, that I'm glad you loved him for a little while."

"Can't we forget him?"

"No. I don't think we'll ever see him again, but I'd like to salvage something and keep it. Don't judge him. You can't judge him, because you never knew the whole story. Neither did I; I only came in towards the end, but I saw enough of his mother, and of his life with her, to understand why he did what he did – in the way that he did it."

"He wanted—"

"He wanted you. His letters after you'd said you would marry him were all but lunatic. He wanted you and he wanted the house he was born in and brought up in. Not at once, but when it came to him in due course, after his mother's death. I think – and I've had a lot of time for thinking since I last saw you – that he must have begun to worry about Lotty before his mother spoke to him about leaving her a share in the house. She was so obviously making her home there – for ever. I'm not sure that his suggestion about her painting seriously wasn't a hint, a hope that she'd take it up, go to a school in London or abroad, get away and perhaps stay away. But she didn't. She simply turned her part of the house into a studio – as you saw. All Grant was doing, in his own way, was what I did at last in my way – that is, prise Lotty out. I don't think I would have been able to do that if she hadn't lost that letter."

"What did the letter have to do with it?"

"It was written nearly eight years ago, but she had treasured it – I thought. But when she told me she'd lost the letter, she showed so little emotion that I realized she'd forgotten – or almost forgotten. She had been happy with Geoff, and she was young, and she had come out of the shadows. She didn't really feel the loss of the letter – and what appalled me was the realization that she hadn't the faintest idea of what would have happened if it had got into Mrs. Tennant's hands."

"But you didn't realize that it had?"

"No. It's clear that I read detective fiction for pleasure – not for profit. The clues built up, one by one – and I missed them all. I saw them, without seeing their significance. Perhaps I was thinking of you. Perhaps not. It wasn't until the end that I could look back and realize that I had seen the beginning. And the beginning, of course, was the letter. But when I saw it, I didn't recognize it."

She turned to look at him. He was staring at the pane of glass that separated them from the driver, and his voice had become dreamy.

"I was there that morning, you see. Grant and I were there, at Spenders. It was snowing, and my visit was short and not sweet, because I had run into the worst-yet row with Mrs. Tennant. She had turned Ronnie out and she was going to hang on to Lotty and Paul, with a share in the house thrown in as additional weight. I told her it was a nice plan, but I'd see to it that it didn't work. Then it was my turn to be booted out. I looked for Grant but couldn't locate him. Then Mrs. Peel told me that he was looking for some papers which she'd been asked to find, and which Grant had told her would be among Lotty's papers. She'd asked Lotty if she might look, and Lotty said yes – but Mrs. Peel had asked Grant to go, because she was sick of searching. As I was ready for the road, I went outside, because it was the quickest way of getting hold of Grant – if you remember, the desk in Lotty's sitting-room had a window on either side of it and—"

"Yes, I remember."

"Well, I approached from the side of the house. In summer, the gravel would have scrunched and the windows would have been open and he would have seen me. But the windows were closed and there was a snow bank preventing me from leaning over and knocking on the window, and I didn't care to shout and risk being heard by his mother – so I decided to go inside again. But in the short time – not more than a moment or two – that I stood there, I saw that he was reading a letter. I could see it, and him, clearly. But after eight years, and in a state of rage, and in a hurry, and standing in snow, and loathing the house and longing to be away from it . . . a man doesn't, in those circumstances, say to himself: 'Why, Grant's reading that letter from Paul that Lotty showed me seven or eight years ago.' All I was thinking of was getting away – and so I went into the house, said I was sorry I'd had another clash with his mother – and left. When you saw me looking for the letter, I was simply trying to make sure that it wasn't anywhere where anybody could lay hands on it. Even when you mentioned the letter in the hospital, things didn't fall into place. And when they did, I could only feel that Grant had acted as he did because it seemed to him the only way to ensure that one day you and he would live at Spenders. And now it's over, and Grant . . . How did you tell him?"

"I drove to Spenders last night. He was alone. I said I'd found out that I didn't love him and that I loved you. And that was all. And if I seem to say harsh things about him, you'll have to forgive me, because it's just to . . . to make it easier."

"To make it easier to forget him?"

"No. To bear it. He wanted the house, and he was there, alone in it. He didn't know that I knew the truth or that you knew the truth or that Mrs. Peel knew the truth. He only knew that the house was his. And he looked . . ." She turned to him and let the tears pour unregarded – "he looked dead. Doomed. He knew what I was going to say. I said it, and I went away – ran. Ran out to the car and drove away and left him there alone in his house. It" – she let him wipe away her tears – "it seemed such a terrible price to pay for what he did. Just to slip a letter into an envelope . . . Richard, where is the letter now?"

"It's buried with Corinne. She saw the beginning; she watched Paul and Lotty fall in love. She was with Lotty when she learned of his death. Nobody should ever have read that letter but Lotty. Nobody ever will again. Grant will go to Canada, and if you want my guess I'd say that Mrs. Peel will follow him there."

"Will she ever tell him?"

"I don't think so. Claire, Claire – my darling——"

She was in his arms. The driver glanced at them now and then in his mirror and thought of his wife and four children, and sighed.

"I love you, Claire."

She was weeping, so that it was difficult to hear what she said in reply. It was, he discovered at last, a request for the loan of a handkerchief; her spare ones, she explained, were on their way to Paris.

CORONET FOR ROMANTIC FICTION

Elizabeth Caddell

☐	16072 1	The Friendly Air	25p
☐	16073 X	Sugar Candy Cottage	25p
☐	17310 6	Home For the Wedding	30p
☐	02791 6	The Lark Shall Sing	30p
☐	12797 X	The Golden Collar	20p
☐	18626 7	The Haymaker	30p

Denise Robins

☐	15084 X	The Unlit Fire	30p
☐	15110 2	Shatter The Sky	30p
☐	02795 9	The Strong Heart	30p
☐	19473 1	This Spring Of Love	35p

Hermina Black

☐	18301 2	Dangerous Masquerade	30p
☐	18781 6	Shadows Of Roses	30p

All these books are available at your bookshop or newsagent, or can be ordered direct from the publisher. Just tick the titles you want and fill in the form below.

CORONET BOOKS, P.O. Box 11, Falmouth, Cornwall.

Please send cheque or postal order, no currency, and allow the following for postage and packing:

1 book – 10p, 2 books – 15p, 3 books – 20p, 4-5 books – 25p, 6-9 books – 4p per copy, 10–15 books – 2½p per copy, 16–30 books – 2p per copy, over 30 books, free within the U.K.
Overseas – please allow 10p for the first book and 5p per copy for each additional book.

Name ....

Address ....

....